Donna Kauffman

SIMON SAYS...

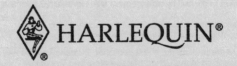

HARLEQUIN®

TORONTO • NEW YORK • LONDON
AMSTERDAM • PARIS • SYDNEY • HAMBURG
STOCKHOLM • ATHENS • TOKYO • MILAN • MADRID
PRAGUE • WARSAW • BUDAPEST • AUCKLAND

Recycling programs
for this product may
not exist in your area.

ISBN-13: 978-0-373-79558-1

SIMON SAYS...

ABOUT THE AUTHOR

USA TODAY bestselling author Donna Kauffman is a former RITA® Award finalist who has seen her books reviewed in venues ranging from *Kirkus Reviews* to *Library Journal* to *Entertainment Weekly*, as well as excerpted in periodicals like *Cosmopolitan*. She lives just outside of the nation's capital in the lovely Virginia countryside, where her nest has emptied of children but seems to rapidly be filling back up with an eclectic menagerie that includes Zazu, a bossy little parrot, and Rufus the mutant catfish. Donna and her menagerie love to hear from readers. You can contact her through her Web site, www.donnakauffman.com.

Books by Donna Kauffman

HARLEQUIN BLAZE
18—HER SECRET THRILL
46—HIS PRIVATE PLEASURE
69—AGAINST ALL ODDS

To Mary and Rhonda,
for your unwavering friendship and support.
I'm a very lucky girl.

1

SOPHIE MAPLETHORPE PAUSED to look at the naked man sprawled across the hotel bed. Even in the early morning darkness, she immediately understood why her best friend had gone to bed with the complete stranger. Maybe not why she'd done so after her own bachelorette party, but if the bottom half of him was as glorious as the broad shoulders and muscled arms presently splayed across the white linen sheets, not to mention all that thick, dark hair curling against his neck… well, even Sophie might have toyed with the idea of risking her entire future for one last fling.

Except you are risking your entire future. And she hadn't even gotten the hot sex first.

Tearing her gaze away from the bed and the naked man, Sophie took another second to let her eyes adjust to the dim interior of Room 706, king, no smoking. Delia said her cell phone had likely fallen out on one of the chairs while she'd been straddling— Sophie shut that image down immediately. But her gaze was drawn to the bed again. And the man presently in it. Daniel Templeton. Investment capitalist, in Chicago for a few meetings. And, apparently not averse to mixing a little consensual pleasure with business.

She sighed. Just a bit. Yes, she'd been focusing on her job

to the point where, maybe, just possibly, her personal life had suffered a little. Okay, a lot. As in she didn't presently have one. Still, even if she wasn't ignoring certain needs for the sake of more important, immediate goals, any normal, red-blooded woman would look at that back, and that backside, clearly and quite deliciously outlined under that casually tangled sheet, and wish, just for a fleeting moment anyway, that she'd been the one doing the hot chair tango last night. All night, according to Delia. The man had stamina. And just because Sophie had to stifle another longing sigh didn't mean she was sex starved or anything.

No, that, apparently, was her best friend's problem.

Well, not anymore.

Sophie resolutely dragged her attention back to the pair of standard hotel chairs arranged in front of the wall-sized picture window, presently hidden behind heavy hotel drapes. She had approximately fifteen minutes to find that damn phone, sneak back out of the room and deliver it to her best friend, before Delia's fiancé made his daily and perfectly punctual 7:00 a.m. morning phone call. Delia's fiancé being Adam Wingate, of the Chicago hotel magnate Wingates. The Wingates who happened to own the chain of hotels she was presently breaking and entering in. The very same hotel chain that employed her as a newly promoted night manager.

She didn't have a pocket in the pants she'd changed into after her shift was over, so she slipped the lanyard holding her master key card back over her neck for the time being, and tiptoed toward the chairs, trying not to think about the fact that she was risking that very promotion, not to mention possible arrest, and God knew what else, all for a damn cell phone.

The instant Delia finished her morning call with her soon-to-be groom, Sophie planned a little lecture of her own. Not that she didn't understand Delia's last-minute bout of cold feet. She'd been telling her friend for, well, almost as long as she'd been dating him, that Adam Wingate was a possessive control freak who, from their very first date, had been categorically programming every last bit of fun and spontaneity out of Sophie's normally bubbly and vibrant best friend.

Delia had countered with the fact that Adam adored her and put her on a pedestal and was just trying to help her improve her social graces so that she could move about in his world. Delia had been all starry-eyed over the fact that someone as important and handsome as Adam Wingate would notice someone in such a lowly position as restaurant hostess. Even if Delia had worked her way up to floor manager of De Trop, which was now one of the hottest spots in Chicago. Which happened to also be in the Wingate Hotel. Delia had earned the position, but Sophie couldn't help but wonder what someone like Adam saw in Delia. Not because of the inequity of their relative bank balances, but because of who they were as people. The obvious answer to everyone else—everyone who was gushing over Delia's fairy-tale Cinderella story—was that of course Adam had fallen in love with Delia's fresh-faced beauty, determined optimism and vivacious personality. Who wouldn't?

And Sophie agreed. Or would have. Except it didn't seem like he really admired those qualities. Other than the beautiful part. Sophie couldn't help but think that maybe Adam really wanted someone he could control with his power, his prestige, and yes, his good looks. Someone not on equal footing. Someone he could constantly remind that it was only through his continued admiration, generosity and—most importantly— approval, that she was enjoying such a wondrous, entitled existence.

Delia hadn't really wanted to hear that. Who would? But what were best friends for?

A little breaking and entering, apparently, Sophie thought as she carefully slid her hand down alongside the seat cushion. Nothing. She tried the other side, thinking that Delia was going to have to listen to her now. The wedding was a week away and clearly her friend was not as confident about the lifetime commitment she was about to make as she'd been so adamantly trying to convince Sophie she was.

Bingo! She pulled out the hard plastic lump, only to discover it was the remote for the television. Great. She tossed it on the seat cushion and scooted over to the other chair and started her systematic search there. She glanced at the glowing red numbers on the bedside stand. Twelve minutes to seven. Super.

She renewed her efforts on the second chair. Scooting closer, she dug deeper, then deeper still, only to find— She pulled out a pair of black string bikinis. "Ew," she said, flinging them instinctively before she could check the reflex action.

"What, you don't like black?"

Sophie froze. *Shit, shit, shit.* But even though her brain was threatening to go into full-blown panic mode, there was another part of her that couldn't help but react to that voice. A much lower part. Delia hadn't mentioned the accent. My God, a body like that *and* an accent?

Focus, Sophie. Caught red-handed—or black-silk-handed anyway—she forced her lips to curve into what she hoped was a friendly smile and slowly looked over her shoulder. "I can explain," she began, without the faintest actual idea of how she was going to do that. But whatever else she might have babbled remained unspoken as she got her first look at his face.

Dark eyes went with that thick rumpled hair, along with serious five o'clock shadow ghosting an incredibly rugged jaw—and was that a cleft in his chin? He was cinema-godlike. Propped up on one elbow, sheet draped across his chest, clutching a scrap of delicate black silk in a hand that was as big and strong looking as the rest of him. Sophie gulped. And keenly felt each second of the past sexless year in every cell of her body. Up until that moment, she'd been perfectly fine making do with a few double A batteries, some well constructed fantasies and, okay, maybe the occasional Matthew McConaughey film fest.

Now?

She swallowed again, against a suddenly parched throat.

He dangled the panties by one long index finger. "Not yours, then?"

What, did he have a harem of women in and out of here? Maybe he'd gotten so drunk last night on the tequila shooters Delia had claimed were the instrument of her demise that he thought she was the one he'd bedded last night.

"Actually," Sophie said, brazening it out. "I lost my cell phone. I think it's in the cushion here. I was trying not to disturb you."

"Interesting."

What was that accent? British?

Her hand involuntarily gripped the master key card around her neck out of habit. She blanched, praying he didn't notice it. She wasn't in uniform, so no little gold name badge on her chest—thank God!—but her ID was dangling on the same lanyard with the key card, the very same lanyard that had the hotel name stitched into it, clearly marking her as someone who worked there.

Shifting so that the clutched tags were shielded as much as possible, she said, "I'm sure it's right here. I'll— Just let me find it and you can get back to sleep."

She held her breath, hoping, praying, he was hungover enough, and groggy enough with sleep, that he took her casually stated request at face value and face planted back into the sheets. Maybe by the time he truly woke up and roused himself out of bed, he'd wonder if he'd dreamed the whole thing. That was if he remembered it at all.

Problem was, even in the early morning gloom, he didn't look too hungover. And other than that delicious rasp to his voice, he didn't sound all that groggy, either. In fact, despite the tousled hair and shadowed jaw, he looked remarkably well rested for a guy who'd just gone to sleep a few hours ago at best. And that after some very—very—energetic sex. If Delia were to be believed, anyway.

Sophie squinched her face a little, digging her hand farther down alongside the cushion. The clock was ticking, and whatever she ended up having to tell this Daniel Templeton in order to talk her way out of his room, none of it was going to mean anything unless she found that damn phone and got it to Delia in the next— She glanced at the clock. Crap! Nine minutes!

But then he was sitting up and the sheet was falling farther down his ridiculously beautiful chest to pool at his perfectly narrow hips. He tossed the panties to the foot of the bed. "Perhaps I could be of some assistance."

Sophie's throat closed over, even as her body hummed with quite a few ideas on exactly how he could very personally assist her. "No, really, don't trouble yourself. After all, you've, ah, done quite...enough." She would have tried for a flirty laugh, or something else that a morning-after lover might have done. If she'd had a clue what that was.

She shoved her hand down even farther and rooted frantically around. "Really, it'll just be a moment and I'll be out of here. I—uh, didn't mean to stay. You know, I know it's not like that, I just—" If she didn't find the damn thing in the next—five minutes!—the ringing of Adam's incoming call would tell her exactly where it was.

At least it would be Sophie answering the call and not some strange man, as Delia had feared. She'd just tell Adam that Delia had accidentally left it in her office last night when she'd stopped by after closing the club, and Sophie was planning on dropping it off this morning on her way home. Yeah, that sounded plausible. He'd be pissy, because he hated anything altering his very specific schedule, but she doubted he'd call the wedding off because of it. Which would have been highly likely if the man presently staring at her with a rather bemused look on his drop-dead gorgeous face had answered the phone instead.

Then Sophie had another idea. What if Delia was wrong? What if the phone hadn't dropped out into the cushions when they'd been playing cowgirl and bucking bronco? Given the way Delia had described them entering the room, clawing each other's clothes off, the phone could really have fallen off Delia's belt clip anywhere.

She scanned the room, half-tempted to rip open the curtains so she could see better, only that would give Mr. Sexy Voice a better opportunity to see what she looked like…and possibly remember she wasn't the same woman he'd dragged home from the bar last night.

"Not that I mind waking up to find a beautiful woman crawling around my hotel room floor, but might I ask how you got in here?"

She should have been scrambling for a good answer, but her brain had gotten stuck on *he thinks I'm beautiful?* Of course, there was very little light. And the guy was obviously a horrible womanizing bar troll. Except she'd never once seen a bar troll who looked like this guy.

"I—uh." She hesitated, then tried to bat her eyelashes. "Don't you recall? I think I'm a tiny bit insulted here." God, she sounded like a bubble-brain moron. No guy would fall for that. Except maybe a bar troll.

She silently prayed and kept on digging. One glance at the clock had her blanching. Three minutes. In three minutes, her friend's fairy-tale marriage to Chicago's wealthiest bachelor was going to go up in smoke, and Sophie's hard won career advancement was going to go down in ignominious flames. And she only had herself to blame.

It had been her idea to have the non-Wingate-sanctioned stealth bachelorette party for Delia in the first place. They'd had it early in the evening, since both Sophie and Delia were supposed to report for work that night. Only Sophie made it in, but when she'd left Delia and some of their friends in the pub, her friend had assured her she'd covered her shift, using a last-minute wedding emergency as an excuse.

Sophie wasn't entirely sure doing tequila shooters with an out-of-town investor—who just happened to be staying at the Wingate!—was exactly an emergency, but she'd trusted that no one would find out, given any Wingate worth their trust fund wouldn't have been caught dead at a local pub anyway. Of course, how the two of them had left the pub and gotten up to this room in the hotel at some point last night without anyone seeing a very drunk Delia, Sophie had no idea. She could only assume Mick, their concierge, had played a large role there, given he shared her views on Delia's Prince Charming, and the fact that there had been nary a whisper along the very healthy hotel grapevine by the time her best friend had found her an hour ago, just as Sophie was getting off shift. She'd arrived in Sophie's office still wearing the same outfit she'd been wearing the evening before, hungover, contrite, crying...and begging Sophie to help her out of a jam.

In hindsight, Sophie should have left well enough alone and let the Wingate's official bachelorette party be the standard-bearer. Adam's sisters were planning a stunning bash for their beloved brother's bride-to-be this very evening, with a guest list anyone would drool over. A guest list that did not include any of Delia's actual friends, of course, but...minor detail. Those would be the same friends she'd had increasingly little time for over the past six months, anyway, as the wedding plans had kicked into high gear, and the Wingate clan had slowly absorbed Delia into the fold. Assimilating her. Like the Borg.

"I beg your pardon," Mr. Sexy Accent said, jolting her back to the moment at hand. He was sitting on the side of the bed now, sheet at his waist, well-toned calves braced apart and manly feet planted on the bedside carpet. "No insult intended, but are you claiming we…know one another?"

Sophie was no actress, but she gave it her best shot. "I'm hurt you've so quickly forgotten. Must be the tequila."

"Tequila? Never touch the stuff. Unless, perhaps, you're referring to your proclivities?" He leaned forward and braced his arms on his knees, so he could get a closer look at her.

Sophie shrank back, but the angle of her hand, presently buried elbow deep in seat cushion, kept her from scooting away.

"Because, tequila or no, I'd have remembered you."

A sliver of daylight speared the crease between the curtains. Just enough to illuminate his face more fully when he leaned forward. Green eyes. He had dark green eyes. And thick lashes. So unfair. No one should get all the goods in one package.

She tried to keep her gaze from dipping to what goods he might have in his other…package. Maybe he wasn't so gifted there. Maybe that was the karmic balance. All that perfection on the outside, but then when you unwrapped it… Except Delia had been pretty specific about…things.

Things Sophie wished her friend had never, ever mentioned. Ever.

Things that made her wish she'd been the one to go pub crawling in the wee hours with the rest of the gang as the party had wound down, instead of having to report to work for her shift. Things that made her wish she'd ended the night doing tequila shooters flat on her back on some sticky, nasty bar while some guy licked salt from around her navel.

Specifically this guy.

Her gaze dipped to his mouth and her own went dry.

"Tequila does crazy things," she said.

"I'm beginning to believe that, yes."

Suddenly there was a knock on the door, making Sophie jump, then freeze. Now what? Room service probably. Great.

If whoever was delivering recognized her, and there was a better than average chance of that happening, she was well and truly screwed. *Like you're not already.*

Then she noted that his entire demeanor had changed. No longer smiling, the muscles across his chest and shoulders tensed—and even more clearly defined—he grabbed the sheet and dragged it around his hips as he stood. "Don't move."

Sophie looked up—way up—to where he towered, Roman godlike, over her, and was pretty sure she couldn't have moved even if she'd wanted to. He was quite intense and very serious, his amusement regarding her unexpected presence completely gone now.

The knock came again, quite loud and insistent, and Sophie automatically found herself thinking she'd have to speak to the room service manager about tempering the enthusiasm of the delivery staff. Or maybe—what if it was someone coming to see him who didn't need to discover him with a woman in his room? A coworker, or worse, a girlfriend...or a wife!

Sophie watched him stride to the door, then she glanced frantically around the room, her gaze landing on the connecting door between rooms. She could use her key and be through that door in a flash. Or course, she risked rousing whoever was in the adjoining room, but a few quickly made apologies and a fast escape into the hall might still be a better strategy than staying in this room another minute longer and facing... whatever it was she was about to face.

Surely he wouldn't give chase wrapped in a bedsheet.

Except, she hadn't found the cell phone yet. Well, maybe it was for the best. Delia was simply going to have to face the consequences of her actions after all. Sophie winced as she tried to imagine the very public spectacle that consequence was likely to be, given the level of attention being paid to what everyone was calling the most romantic wedding of the year. The tycoon and the cocktail waitress. Despite Delia not having been one for years. Nightclub manager apparently didn't make nearly as good a headline.

Sophie slid her hand from the cushion. Maybe they'd both luck out and the battery would have died and it wouldn't ring. Then she could come back in here later after he checked out and do a more thorough search before housekeeping did their thing. But in order to do that, she had to get out of here. Right now. And pray like hell he didn't complain to hotel security...and that he checked out while the day staff was still on duty.

She was just starting to inch her way across the floor, when he stepped back into the room.

"And where might you be going?"

"Really, I'll get out of your hair. I don't need my phone that badly. Just, if you find it, would you turn it off and leave it on the dresser? The cleaning staff will find it and turn it in and it will all be okay and—" She was babbling.

But that came to an abrupt stop when she finally turned and looked at him.

He was standing in the space where the hallway opened into the bedroom. The sheet was tucked low around his hips. In one hand, he held a white envelope that she recognized as hotel stationery.

In the other hand, he held a gun.

2

SIMON LASSITER HAD A NUMBER of concerns at the moment, each carefully accounted for, each with a plan of action in place. Every move he made while he was here in Chicago had to run like a perfectly crafted Swiss timepiece. There was no room for error. One mistake, and all would be lost.

He looked at the woman presently perched on the chair in his hotel room, and tried to tell himself she wasn't that fatal mistake.

He certainly hadn't accounted for her. And there was no plan in place to deal with something like this.

But Simon hadn't gotten to this point in life by being a pessimist. According to the note he'd just received, one he'd paid handsomely to have delivered instantly, day or night, under any circumstances...Tolliver had checked in. His quarry was on the premises. Finally, it was all coming together. Not that getting his hands on the Shay Emerald was going to be easy, but he was a damn sight closer now than he'd been before. And it was a certainty that he'd never have a chance again.

Which had him thinking that, perhaps, the hotel key card currently dangling from his surprise guest's lovely neck might be of great assistance in that endeavor.

"Mr. Templeton," she blurted, her gaze fixed on the gun in his hand. "Really, I don't think that's necessary."

"This?" He wiggled the barrel slightly, making her tense further. "I believe you broke into my room. I'm merely protecting myself." He frowned, then. "Who's Templeton?"

"Daniel Templeton?"

He slowly shook his head.

"Seriously?"

"Quite."

Her chin dropped, along with her shoulders. She closed her eyes and swore quietly. "All this, and I snuck into the wrong damn room. This is 706, right?"

He nodded.

"If the Wingates don't kill her, I'm going to kill her myself."

Simon didn't understand what she was muttering about, but whatever had pissed her off wasn't his problem. Getting into Tolliver's room and stealing—retrieving—the emerald before it went on display at the Art Institute Museum this weekend, that was his problem. "Have a seat," he told her, motioning to the chair behind her with the gun barrel. "We need to have a little talk."

"Do you really need to point that gun at me? I assure you, I'm not dangerous. Just let me go and we can pretend we never met."

"Ah, but you did pretend we'd met. In fact, you wanted me to believe we'd had something of a fling. Under the influence of tequila, I believe you said."

She didn't respond to that, squirming a little in her seat instead. So, she was game to be bold—her presence in his room was evidence enough of that—but when pushed, she really wasn't a very good liar. Good to know.

"Of course, you thought I was a certain Mr. Templeton. Just how many men's rooms do you visit every night?" He motioned to the key card. "Perhaps in America, a five-star hotel provides a level of personal service we don't typically experience in London hotels of the same caliber."

"London?" Her brow furrowed. "You are British, then? Because you don't really sound—"

"English? It's home currently, but I'm native Kiwi. New Zealand," he added, when her brow wrinkled even further. And why on earth was he telling her any of this? Was it those oh-so-wide gray eyes? Or perhaps it was the combination of the strawberry blond curls and milkmaid skin. Skin that hadn't been baked or painted within an inch of its life, as most American women seemed to favor. Innocence. She projected it. And yet, here she sat, in his room, without invitation.

Simon well knew that looks could not only be deceiving, they often were. In fact, these days, he'd come to bank on that fact, and used it for his own advancement whenever it suited his needs, adopting the Yankee sentiment that if you couldn't beat them, joining them was often the wise alternative. Perhaps he straddled that line a bit, but the premise still worked.

"You should do a better job keeping your...callers straight. Men like to feel as if they're the only one, after all, even if it is a shaky illusion at best."

Those lovely dove-gray eyes widened. "You think I'm a hooker?"

"You sneak into a man's room and start digging around the furnishings looking for a purported cell phone. Not on the bedside table or dresser, but wedged down in a chair. You then imply we slept together after an evening spent at least partly consuming an ambiguous quantity of alcohol, and call me by some other bloke's name. Which, in my book, means one of two things."

She folded her arms and, for the first time, he saw a spark of defiance. Albeit, barely more than a flicker. After all, he was holding a gun on her.

"And those two things would be?"

"One, you had a fling with a gentleman who was in this room prior to me and are only now tracking back to where you might have lost your phone." He leaned against the wall, careful to keep the gun poised and aimed at her. "Or two, you broke into my room to steal something from me and the rest was just a clever ruse to make me think you're not really a common thief."

"Why would I steal something from you? I thought you were Daniel Templeton. I don't even know you."

"You apparently don't know Mr. Templeton well, either, if you didn't know I wasn't him." He tugged at the sheet tucked around his waist. "Or perhaps it's some other part of Mr. Templeton you'd recognize."

Her mouth dropped open in instant offense, which both heartened and amused him. Because while he honestly had no idea why she was there, the fact remained, she was. He was fairly certain that key card hanging around her neck was a master key, as it was the most likely way she could have gotten into his room. Which meant she was probably employed here, and though the Wingate's extensive marketing campaign wanted you to believe they could anticipate their guests' every need, he doubted those of the more carnal variety were on that catered-to list.

Clearly, she'd ignored more than a few rules. All of which was in his favor, as a passkey to any room in the hotel—one in particular that he had in mind—could come in very, very handy right about now.

If only her skill at lying was a bit more sharply tuned, he might be able to use her in a few other ways, as well.

"So, if you are neither thief nor…gentleman's companion, then please explain why you are here, uninvited."

"I told you. I was trying to retrieve a phone. And the reason I didn't recognize you, or that this wasn't the right room, was because I'm not retrieving *my* phone, it's my friend's phone."

"Ah. Your friend's phone is it now?"

She sighed. "I know that sounds like a cliché, but it's true." She looked at him, as if sizing him up, her gaze clearly wary. "I'll tell you the whole story, but could you please lower the gun? It's not like I can go anywhere or do anything."

He lifted a casual shoulder. "I don't know what you're capable of. What I do know of you is that you are capable of breaking and entering. Not a point in your favor, I might add, so who knows what other lengths you'd go to? Or what other hidden skills or weapons you might have?"

"Please," she said. "I'm just a friend trying to do a friend a favor and get her out of a potential jam with her fiancé. Which, since I trusted her to remember which room she was in, by now has already exploded in her face, as I didn't get the phone back in time. Trust me, I don't make a habit of breaking into strange men's rooms, or any rooms. It was a one-time thing, which I only did out of desperation, and because I felt a little responsible for getting her into a situation where she might use bad judgment, which, you know, boy, did she."

Simon listened to her sudden explosion of chatter with one ear tuned to how he could use the information to his advantage, and another ear just, well, amused by her. She was certainly unlike any woman of his acquaintance. "It's so implausible, I actually want to believe you."

She heaved out a sigh of relief and started to stand up. "Great, thank you. And I promise I won't tell anyone that you have a gun, which I completely understand, by the way. You can't be too safe when traveling, and I'm sure it's registered to you and all that, and, of course, we could always hold it in the hotel safe for you, but then, I guess that would defeat the purpose of having one in case of…well…"

"Someone breaking into my room?" He couldn't help it, he smiled. She was quite something when rattled. She was quite something, period.

"Right," she said on a half laugh, even as she blushed quite prettily in embarrassment. She edged away from the chair. "And please accept my apologies for starting your day off like this. If I can do *anything* to make it up to you—" Her eyes widened when his smile spread to a grin. "I mean, not *anything* anything, but, you know, anything within reason. Or maybe just letting me go and pretending we never met is enough. I'd be fine with that. Whatever you think is best, really. I'll just be going and—"

He waved the gun casually, motioning her back to the chair. "What I think is best is that you sit back down and we talk about how you might make it up to me."

Her throat worked, and she wetted her lips. He was surprised to feel his body respond to the sight of that pink tongue and those lips that he was only now realizing had a rather kewpie-shaped bow to them. Quite delectable really.

"Is that really necessary? I mean, I'm sure you have important things to do—" She nodded jerkily at the envelope he still had in his other hand. "And I would be happy to make myself scarce. You'll never see me again. I promise."

He forced his thoughts away from watching those lips move and back to the moment at hand. "Indeed, I do have important things to do, and I think you can be of some assistance with that."

Her gaze dipped to the sheet wrapped at his waist, and his body responded with another twitch of awareness. Best to get them off that path as soon as possible. That was the last kind of distraction he needed at the moment. No matter what his body would have him believe. "I assure you, I am not looking for those kinds of favors." He waited until she mercifully looked back at his face. "What would be more helpful in the way of making up for this…disturbance, would be that you extend your life of crime to include one more round of breaking and entering."

She frowned now, clearly surprised by the request. "What do you mean?"

He motioned to the key card dangling between her breasts.

"Can you please not wave that around?" she asked. "In fact, can we agree you don't really need that anymore?"

"Not quite yet. When I can keep the odds stacked in my favor, I do."

"So...what do you want, then? I can't give you this key."

He leaned against the wall, wrapping one arm around his waist and bracing his other elbow on it to keep the gun steady. "Really?" Because he was thinking she might be persuaded to let him have the key. When she wet her lips again, his body decided maybe he could convince her to give up a few other things, as well. He ignored his body. Now was not the time. Nor was she his type. She'd come into his life as trouble, and he was pretty certain that was what she'd always be.

"Really," she said, though her voice was a bit unsteady.

He wiggled the gun when she started to argue. "Not only am I holding encouragement for you to do just that, but even if I wasn't, I have the weapon of knowledge. I don't know who you are or where you came by that key, but I imagine hotel security would be quite interested to know of its whereabouts and usage in the past hour."

She sat a bit more rigidly in her seat, but didn't answer.

"I'll take that as a yes."

"Two wrongs don't make a right. I know what I did wasn't ethical, but it was for a good cause and no one was harmed in any way. Still, I should have been more direct. Just knocked on the door and disturbed a guest at the crack of dawn...or—or something. But I won't compound my bad judgment by doing something even more wrong."

"Unfortunately, it's the only thing you have that I want."

Her gaze dipped down again, and he would have sworn a brief flash of insult crossed her face. He hadn't intended the slight, but perhaps it was just as well she believed he had.

He drew her attention upward. "How do you know I don't

want to use it for some benevolent reason? Such as the one you purportedly had?"

"Because you carry a gun. I only carry a key."

"Both pretty powerful weapons," he pointed out. "Both capable of creating leverage where none might otherwise exist. And of getting the user into unplanned trouble when mismanaged." He lowered the gun. "In my case, my weapon has a safety, to keep bad things from inadvertently happening. I'm assuming your key didn't come with a similar safeguard." He smiled. "More's the pity for you." He tucked the hotel stationery under his arm, then stuck out his free hand. "I promise I'll turn it back in to you. Unless, of course, anything should happen. Say, you run and tell someone I'm a bad guy with a gun and a passkey. Then all bets are off."

"Are you?" she asked. "A bad guy, I mean? Isn't this where you tell me you work for Interpol, or some hush-hush government agency, and by giving you my passkey, I'll be helping to maintain national security?"

"No, nothing so exciting as all that." His smile spread to a grin. "Although, as cover stories go, that one is quite good. I'll have to remember it."

"So…who are you, then? And why do you need a master passkey?"

"Those are probably questions it's best you don't have the answers to. You'll have to trust me."

"Like you trust me?"

"Look at it this way. We'll both have something on the other that is likely to keep us in line. What better measure of trust is there?"

"That's blackmail, not trust."

He just shrugged.

"Whose room do you want to get into?"

"More information you don't need to know."

"I will if I'm going to help you get into it."

He cocked a brow. "So you agree to help me, then?"

She nodded at the gun. "I hardly see where I have a choice."

He didn't believe her innocent face, not for a second. More likely she was hoping to learn as much as possible so she could find a way to get out, and report him. He wiggled the fingers of his still outstretched hand. "I'll return the key when I'm done."

"My trust doesn't extend that far. For my own future protection, I need to know where it was used. The key and I stay together."

"Except that wouldn't protect you. Quite the opposite. If something goes awry with my...mission, you can honestly disavow any knowledge of how it was used, as you truly won't know. It's to your advantage to hand it over. And if it's not actually yours, then you can step out of the chain of ownership completely. I won't point the finger at you and I can leave it wherever it would best suit your needs for someone to find it when I'm done. I think that's a very fair trade."

"Just show me where you want to go and I'll let you in, then keep the key on me. We part ways and no one is the wiser. On either side."

"Then you'd be a willing accomplice. Not a good thing. You're really not that good on this whole criminal acts thing, are you?"

"I told you. This is an aberration. I'm the Goody Two-shoes of my group, trust me. It was a wild act of rebellion for me just to stage the damn stealth bachelorette party in the first place."

He half-laughed. "The goodie-what?"

"Never mind."

"Sounds like you're rather making a new sport out of rebellious behavior. Although what a stealth bachelorette party is, I couldn't hope to fathom." He held up his hand. "And don't wish to."

"You can mock me all you want, but I'm not giving you the

key. If something goes awry, as you said, and I'm implicated in any way, then I'll tell them you forced me, threatened me. Given the gun, I think I'll be perfectly believable. So, give me the room number and let's go."

Under other circumstances he might have found her adorably stubborn, but at the moment, he wasn't so amused. "I won't be using it immediately. So I will take the key now… or you can prepare to be my guest for a while."

Her gaze narrowed. "How long is 'a while'?"

He shrugged. "A day or two, probably, at the most."

"You can't keep me here that long," she exclaimed.

"I don't see why not. The hotel offers very nice room service. You'll live in relative comfort, lend me the key when it's needed, then we'll part ways."

"I have a job, friends, a wedding. I'll be missed."

Now his eyes widened. "So, was it your *own* party you were arranging, then?" He couldn't say why the news disappointed him so. Considering he wasn't planning on doing anything with her other than obtaining her helpful little key card, it didn't matter if she was already otherwise involved. And yet the thought didn't make him happy.

"My best friend is getting married this weekend. Sunday. Here. In the hotel. It was her phone I was trying to retrieve."

"Ah." He smiled as the puzzle pieces began to align themselves. "Well, perhaps you won't have to concern yourself with that if that unanswered call was as important as you say. And, think of it, you'll be out of the line of fire, which might be to your advantage given the role you say you played in your friend's downfall."

"Her fiancé is Adam Wingate."

Bloody hell. Simon tried not to visibly react. Of course he couldn't just luck into an easy solution to the job at hand. He had to get a whole handful of new obstacles. "Of the Wingate Hotel Wingates, I presume?"

She nodded. "You know, I'm still okay with just getting up and walking out of here and pretending we never met."

"Good try." He tapped the barrel of the gun against his thigh, sorting through the possibilities. "How close are you with the Wingate family, then?"

"I'm not. My friend is. They aren't big fans of friends from what will soon be her former life, so don't get any ideas." She kept looking at the gun, then back at him. "And after they find out I threw the bachelorette party..." He was surprised to see a rueful smile touching the corners of her mouth when she looked back at him. "You know, on second thought, maybe I will hide out here."

His smile returned. She was an interesting woman, he'd give her that. She had pluck. And heart. She'd broken into a stranger's hotel room for the sake of a friend. He might be able to use that good heart to his advantage.

But he hadn't missed the slight tremor in her fingers. Not quite as insouciant as she'd like him to believe, then.

"If you don't tell me something of what your plans are," she added, "then I don't really have anything on you. You said we'd both have leverage."

"I have the gun. You have the key."

"Guess who wins that matchup? If you're really willing to shoot me, that is."

"You have no idea what I'm capable of."

She shuddered. "Exactly." With a considering look on her face, she looked at the bed.

He followed her gaze, more intrigued than he should be by her sudden interest in that particular part of the room. In fact, he was more intrigued by her than he should be, period. He had never minded working alone, living alone. It suited him, or he'd grown to embrace it, anyway. It was essential to his line of work, at which he excelled. And it made sense to stick with what one was good at, didn't it?

Partners led to problems. Personally and professionally.

That was his motto and nothing that he'd learned in life thus far had encouraged him to change that belief. He certainly had no business changing it now, of all times. For the first time he was operating on his own, not in the employ of someone else. He had this one chance to fix what he'd screwed up, and right a very lamentable wrong.

"Somebody else might," she said, pulling him from his straying thoughts.

"Somebody else might what?"

"Know what you're capable of. The owner of those panties, for instance."

He smiled. "The cleaning staff here might need a bit of prodding to be more thorough in their cleaning."

"Indiana Jones wouldn't have found those panties. I don't even want to know what you were doing to bury them so deep." Her cheeks turned rosy as her unintentional entendre hung out there for a long beat. But she recovered and bulled on with an attempt at a carefree lift of the shoulder. "For all I know you want to get into another guest's room over some woman you're involved with. Is this a domestic situation?"

"Hardly."

"You say that as if you can't imagine a woman being so important."

"Your supposition, not mine," he said, more irritated than he should be by her summation. After all, hadn't he just had the exact same thought?

"So, if it's not a lover or significant other behind all this, then who?"

"Who said it was a who?" He immediately gave himself a swift mental kick. She had this way of easing information out of him when he wasn't paying attention. Those soft curls, big eyes and cupid-bow lips, made it too easy to forget she could potentially ruin everything. He wasn't entirely sure what his plans were going to be, moving forward, but if he didn't get the Shay back under Guinn's deserving ownership first, it might not matter.

"So, you don't want access to someone, you want access to something. But guests generally don't keep anything of great value in their rooms. Anything valuable would be in the hotel safe. Which is well guarded," she hurried to add. "With everyone so concerned these days about security, the whole system was overhauled recently and now uses the latest technology."

"Yes, I believe you offered its protection earlier, for the safekeeping of my leverage here." He wiggled the gun barrel. "So...given your insight into the inner workings of the hotel, including security, I assume that passkey is yours, then?"

The flash that crossed her face was answer enough, but he waited to hear her response. It was a small measure of comfort to know he wasn't the only one having difficulty keeping delicate information under wraps. Except he was the professional here. So it was a surprise when she opted to not risk damning herself further and kept silent. An admirable trait not often seen in the fairer sex, in his experience.

"Well, your having access to the vault does add a new element to the situation," he said. "A good one, I might add."

She looked away and he could see the self-recrimination on her lovely face. She really wasn't having a good day.

Any other time, he'd be sympathetic. In fact, he'd probably have even offered to help her out. More than was probably wise, he'd been the champion of the downtrodden and the underdog when considering which job to take on. His bottom line wasn't often improved by those choices, but he slept better at night, which was a fine trade-off as far as he was concerned. If only he'd followed his gut where Guinn was concerned, who'd quite clearly been the underdog, but with a rather ambiguous claim on the Shay...and not helped Tolliver, with his well-documented claim to the stone, he wouldn't be in his current situation.

But it was precisely because of his current situation that helping her was out of the question. She'd gotten herself into her current predicament by making less-than-wise choices herself. Unfortunately, she was going to have to be left to deal with those consequences. She was handing him a possible solution he couldn't ignore. As a hotel employee with a clear knowledge of hotel security protocol, her unauthorized use of a master key took on even greater significance. Which meant more leverage for him. He had no choice but to use it.

"How do I know you won't turn me in after you get what you want?" she asked.

"You don't."

"Which brings me back to the whole leverage debate. What do I have on you? Who are you? Do you work for the government? Ours, yours, whatever?"

"Nothing so dashing and heroic. What makes you think I'm not just a common, garden-variety thief?"

"There's nothing common about you," she replied, then her cheeks once again flushed the most becoming shade of pink. "I mean, your accent is polished, not street-wise, and you carry yourself quite—" Her flush deepened and she looked away from where her gaze had fixed itself on the lower half of his body. "Never mind." She straightened in her chair and lifted her chin, which would have come across far more effectively if she wasn't still hugging herself around the middle. "So you're a thief. You do this often, then?"

"I'm a recovery specialist." Which was the truth. His job was to find things that people had lost, or had otherwise lost possession of. He only worked for those who could prove a rightful claim on whatever it was they wanted recovered. Of course, he tried, as best as he could, to stay within the bounds of local laws, wherever he happened to be. On the rare occasion he had to tiptoe across that line, the only one who knew the line had been crossed was the one with little room to point a finger. Sophie was an entirely new kind of threat, however. So he had to think this through carefully.

"Who do you work for?"

"Private interests." Very private this time.

"Not a garden-variety thief if you're stealing something from a high-profile hotel."

"You sure ask a lot of questions for someone who doesn't want to be involved."

"Information is power."

"True. What is your name?" He smiled when she looked at him like he was a nutter for asking her to give up such a vital piece of information without coercion. "I should know the name of my partner in crime."

He could see the continued slight tremor in her shoulders and knees, but she held his gaze quite valiantly. "You first," she said, then added, "Gesture of faith."

"You wouldn't know if I was telling the truth."

"Neither will you."

"I could find out easily enough by asking anyone on staff if they recognize the name."

"It's a large hotel with lots of employees. Besides which, I could just check the guest register to see who is in this room."

He nodded, and didn't bother to point out that he could have registered under a fake name. "You can call me Silas." He hadn't been called by that nickname since he'd been a young boy, but he felt better giving her at least something of the truth. He was going to abuse her goodwill quite enough as it was. He had little else to offer in return.

"Sophie," she said, then when he waited a beat longer, she sighed and added, "Maplethorpe." She lifted a shoulder when he raised a brow. "I couldn't make something like that up."

"You're being too modest. It's a lovely name."

She didn't reply, but given he could easily find out more

about her as she was an employee here, and that he'd already established she was a lousy liar, he chose to believe her.

His stomach chose that moment to rumble quietly. He absently rubbed it with his free hand, then remembered the note when it fluttered to the floor. And the rest of the news it had delivered. Tolliver had checked in...but not alone. *Shit.* She really was distracting. "I have some business to attend to," he told her before snagging it off the carpet and walking over to the phone on the bedside stand. "I'll order some room service. I shouldn't be gone long. You can make yourself at home."

"You expect me to just stay in the room while you're gone?"

"I could stop downstairs by security and explain that a hotel employee broke into my room this morning. Or you could enjoy a day off at my expense."

"They'll notice when I don't report for work soon."

She'd looked away when she said that. A complete loss as a liar. He doubted any amount of training would fix it, either. He'd simply have to work around it. "When is your next shift?"

She kept her gaze averted. At least she seemed to realize she wasn't good at it. Or her conscience wouldn't allow it. It amazed him she'd mustered up the gumption to break in at all. He hoped her friend appreciated her act of courage. Somehow he doubted it. Friends who'd ask friends to do something like this rarely appreciated the importance of what they were requesting. Something he was a bit too familiar with. Which was why he was here, cleansing old sins and clearing the slate. He should have seen through Tolliver's philanthropic front to the greed that festered just beneath. And because he hadn't, he'd retrieved—hell, stolen—something from an innocent old man who, by all rights, should still have possession of the priceless artifact Simon had robbed him of.

Guinn had no idea he was here, trying to right that wrong,

but right it he would. For the old man, and for his own redemption.

When she didn't respond, he said, "Well, when the time comes, you may have to call in with some terrible malady that will keep you in bed for a few days." His gaze strayed to the unmade bed, and thoughts of how she could spend those few days flooded his brain with startling clarity and detail. His body responded so swiftly he was forced to step back into the shadows of the hallway. He didn't mind scaring her a little to ensure she'd help, but he didn't need the added distraction of her worrying that he would physically attack her. Better to let her believe what he'd said earlier. That the only thing desirable about her was that passkey.

Then he caught her gaze, also on his unmade bed, and that lovely pink flush had returned to her cheeks…and his body continued its urgent appeal to his baser nature. All those glances at him—all of him—that she'd been unable to defer earlier proved he wasn't the only one with the same diverting thoughts. It probably would have been better if he didn't know that about her. He prided himself on his ability to focus on a task to the exclusion of all outside distractions. It was, in part, why he was so good at his job. But the delightfully spirited and surprisingly tenacious Miss Sophie Maplethorpe was turning out to be quite the temptation.

"So," he said, lifting the phone. "How do you like your eggs?"

"You really can't mean to make me stay here."

He sighed as he took in her defiant, cherubic face and the hands that trembled, now clutching the arms of the padded chair. She and that key of hers would either be his salvation, or his downfall.

So. He had no choice but to ensure it was the former, rather than the latter.

He laid the gun on the nightstand, then casually ripped the clock from the wall and snapped off the electrical cord. The desk phone cord swiftly followed. Couldn't have her calling down to the desk for a quick rescue.

He looped the lengths of both cords around his hand and smiled at her. "I beg to differ. Now, would you prefer to be tied to the chair? Or the bed?"

3

SOPHIE GULPED BUT COULDN'T get it past the knot in her throat. He'd snapped those cords with such casual violence. She realized, perhaps truly for the first time, even after having a gun aimed at her, just how much trouble she was in. He'd seemed so...civilized. Before.

As civilized as a half-naked man who looked and sounded like he could be in the next Bond movie could seem, anyway. It was the accent. So smooth, so polished. With just that hint of Down Under to roughen up his gorgeous edges.

Now all she could do was stare at the swift way he looped those cords around his hand...and wonder how many women he'd tied up before. "I'm— That won't be necessary," she said, forcing herself not to shrink back as he crossed the room toward her. "I'll stay here."

He extended his hand. "Your key."

She instinctively covered it with her hand. "You're going to use it right now? I thought you said—"

"Consider it insurance. I come back, and you're not here, I go immediately to hotel security."

"I could claim you stole it from me."

"They have cameras mounted in the hallways, do they not?

I'm assuming we could prove you entered my room using this key."

"I could come up with a plausible reason for doing that."

"One that precludes you wearing your uniform? And not being seen exiting the room for some time? I'm afraid that the only explanations that work won't paint you in a flattering light. You either snuck in to take something…or you snuck in to get something."

Damn him for making her cheeks heat up like that. She hated being fair complexioned most of the time, but none more so than right now. He'd probably noticed her almost genetic inability to keep from staring at him—but in her defense, he was mostly naked, and an Adonis to boot—and he was using her…her weakness against her. The cad. Of course, he could be using it against her in a far more nefarious way. He could be trying to seduce the damn key from her. But no.

What it said about her that she felt insulted rather than relieved by that little fact, she didn't want to know.

"You go take care of your errand and I'll be here when you get back. Then we can discuss what you want to use the key for and when you plan to use it." There. She'd sounded almost businesslike. Like she worked with gun-wielding thieves all the time. She just wanted to get him out of the room so she could get away from him and figure out what her options were. "As you've pointed out, running wouldn't be a very smart move on my part." Not that she'd made any smart moves thus far this morning, but why stop now?

"The key. Or I secure your presence here in other ways." He dangled the electrical cords. "Primitive, I know, and my apologies. But your company was unexpected and I'm afraid I didn't come prepared."

So damn smooth, that voice, that smile, those eyes. Were ruthless thieves supposed to have kind eyes? And a body made for complete, unadulterated sin?

He wants to steal something from your hotel. Think,

Sophie, think. And what she was thinking was that her only defense against his threatened accusations of breaking into his room—which, of course, happened to be true—would be if she somehow managed to thwart whatever mission he was on, thereby saving the hotel from both the robbery, a possible lawsuit from the guest he planned to steal from and the resulting negative media splash that scenario would provoke.

She'd started the morning with a headache from working all night on too little sleep and too much alcohol, and a very real concern for her best friend's future. Somehow, since then, she'd landed herself in a remake of *It Takes a Thief*. Complete with devastatingly handsome leading man.

"You said trust was built on mutual blackmail," she said, scrambling. She couldn't let him take that key.

"Did I?" The corners of his mouth kicked up in an amused smile that put a little devilish twinkle in his eyes. God, they were so green. Honestly, the gene fairy had just had a field day with this guy.

"More or less. The way I see it, the career I've worked so hard for is in jeopardy." She lifted a hand. "My fault, I know, but other than invading your personal space uninvited, I haven't committed any real crime or hurt anyone. But you could report me and cost me everything. So I'm inclined to help you. Even if you hadn't held a gun on me, though that did make an impression, let me tell you. Not only do I want to protect my job and my reputation, but if I were to run, you know where I work. You could track me down pretty easily. And we both know you're armed and dangerous."

Her gaze dipped to the cords and she stifled an involuntary shudder. She told herself it was the image of him ripping those cords from the wall that caused the reaction, when, if she were really honest, it was the image of him putting those hands on her, for any reason. Pathetic, really, but there it was. If she got out of this in one piece, the first thing she was doing was getting laid. Clearly she'd neglected that part of her personal maintenance for far too long if she was fantasizing over a guy who was threatening to either shoot her or tie her up.

"You don't even need to order room service for me," she went on. Like she could eat anything. But…could it be he was seriously considering her argument? "Probably better we don't take a chance that any of the staff catches me in here anyway."

"Another good point." He cocked his head. "You're a surprise, Sophie Maplethorpe."

"Why do you say that?"

"Well, you have an angelic look about you." His smile grew. "And yet, here you are. Bargaining with an alleged thief."

"I'm just trying to save my job, my future," she said, feeling a bit miffed at his characterization of her. Here she was giving him her femme fatale best, going head to head with Bond II, and he thought she was an innocent angel.

"Perhaps you should have thought of that before you decided to break into a guest's room." He knelt down. "Sorry, love, but you're a flight risk. And that's one risk I can't take."

"But—"

"You keep your key. For now. And I keep you." He nodded. "Palms together."

She gripped her tags more tightly. "What's to keep you from taking my key once you tie me up? Where's the trust here?"

"I suppose you were right about that after all."

"No trust amongst thieves, then?"

His eyes twinkled. "Most unwise, I'd think. But I operate alone, so I can't rightly say."

"So you do admit it, you are a thief."

"Recovery specialist."

"That's clever, but doesn't it mean the same thing?"

"It's the truth, actually."

He moved so suddenly, so smoothly and swiftly she couldn't react until it was too late. He pinned his weight against her knees, preventing her from kicking out at him, while he took her hands, still gripping the tags on her lanyard, and quickly and quite expertly looped the electrical cord around her wrists, binding them just tightly enough that she couldn't wiggle them free. The instant he was done with that, and while she was still reeling—much to her own shame—at the feel of his big, warm hands on her skin, he had them on her ankles. He shifted just enough to loop the cord around them in seconds flat, then cinched them together and tied the remaining cord to the wooden cross bar that connected the legs of the chair to each other.

She tried to kick out, but her heels were snug to the wooden bar. She swung her tied hands at his head, as much out of frustration as anything, but he easily caught them in one fist. "Now, now." He took the loose end of the cord from her wrists and tugged it down, pulling her joined hands between her knees, then, pinning them there, tied the wrist cord to the one at her ankles.

Then he rocked back on his heels, and released her as he stood and moved out of reach. Not that she could swing anything at him at the moment. He walked into the bathroom and came back a moment later with what looked like the belt to a Wingate Hotel bathrobe.

She eyed him warily. "Now what? You've already roped me like a prize heifer. I can hardly go anywhere, or do anything." Which was, unfortunately, quite true. She wriggled against her bonds, but it just made the cords cut more tightly into her skin.

"You still have one weapon left," he told her, and stepped behind her.

She craned her neck, trying in vain to see what he was doing, then felt him kneel behind her chair, his breath fanning the side of her neck. Only she could have a mostly naked man breathing softly against the tender, sensitive skin of her neck, whispering in her ear…so he could explain why he had to gag her with a bathrobe belt.

"I'm truly sorry, but I can't have you yelling out for assistance now, can I?"

To his credit, his hands were gentle and he didn't tie it tightly, just snugly enough that any noise she made was muffled enough not to carry.

He stepped around in front of her.

She glared at him, but didn't give him the satisfaction of trying to scream or kick, much less beg.

"I am sorry." A smile played at his mouth. "But you did get to keep your key."

She might have growled at that. Just a little.

"I promise not to take long." He disappeared into the bathroom. A moment later, she heard the shower come on.

Was he kidding? He'd trussed her up like a holiday turkey, gagged her, and now he was going to take a leisurely shower?

Steam wafted out from beneath the bathroom door. Sophie was pretty certain the same was coming out her ears. What on earth had she been thinking to let Delia talk her into this stupid, cockamamie stunt? Of course, Delia had been crying, half-hysterical and still a little bit drunk at the time, so what was a best friend to do? *Get the right room number, for one,* her little voice mentioned. Sometimes she hated her little voice. Where was it when she'd really needed it? Like when it should have stopped her from kicking her entire career into the gutter, all to retrieve a stupid cell phone because her best friend's fiancé was an asshole whom she shouldn't even be marrying in the first place.

And God only knew what was going on with Delia right this moment. Had Adam called as usual? What was she thinking, of course he had. The man was an android. Had Daniel Templeton, wherever he was, answered the call? Sophie shivered at the very idea. It was quite possible that all holy hell

was being wrought right at this very moment—the Wingate
Wedding of the Century imploding, media swarming, cater-
ers and florists in three states collapsing. And where was she
when her best friend needed her most? Tied to a damn chair
in one of her own hotel rooms, while an incredibly hot thief
stood naked under the shower in the adjoining bath, that's
where.

Her gaze shifted back to the bathroom door, and she hated
herself a little, but even that didn't stop her from imagining what he looked like, all slick and soapy. It's not like she
didn't have a pretty good idea, given she'd seen almost all of
him already. Almost. God. The mental movie went on for a
few more frames before she finally, albeit reluctantly, shut it
down.

She sighed and slumped in the chair, as much as she could
anyway. Truly pathetic.

Her head jerked up when the door opened and he strolled
out in a cloud of steam, a damp hotel towel clinging precari-
ously to his hips, thick black curls matted to his neck.

"Sorry." He stepped to the closet, rooted around, grabbed
some clothes, then ducked back into the bathroom.

"Don't mind me," she muttered through the bathrobe belt,
wishing she hadn't noticed that he'd shaved. The shadow of a
beard had actually been sexier. But now he looked downright
deadly.

She squeezed her eyes shut. Sex. Seriously, the second thing
she was doing when she got loose. Right after she found a
new job. Of course, no hotel in the universe was going to hire
her once word got out. The Wingates would see to that. So,
what if managing a hotel was the only thing she'd ever really
wanted to do?

Thank goodness Grandma Winnifred wasn't alive to witness her downfall. She would be so hurt and disappointed
if she could see her favorite granddaughter right now. Sophie glanced upward and sent a silent prayer of forgiveness,

remembering the smells, sounds and sights of the family restaurant her grandmother had run, the one Sophie had grown up in after the loss of her parents at age nine. Her world had always been filled with people, and conversation, good food and contented smiles. Everyone loved her grandmother, and Winnie's was where people came to relax, to get away from their troubles, to enjoy a good meal, a place where they would always be welcome.

Sophie had known early on that she wanted to create that same world for herself, to carry on in her grandmother's stead, bringing that kind of home away from home to others. She'd also discovered early that cooking was never going to be her forte, but where her palate might fail her, her eye did not. She had a special flair for creating the perfect atmosphere, for managing and hostessing. It was at Winnie's urging that she'd considered her other options, such as running her own inn, providing a different sort of home away from home. And had known immediately it was the perfect dream. But that took money.

So she'd done it the smart way, gone to school, getting her degree in hotel management, working her way up, putting away money, until the time was right to launch her own place, her own way. She'd had Winnie's support, and that of everyone at the restaurant. And though both were gone now, her focus had never wavered, and that was in large part due to the confidence they'd all given her. She'd been a night manager of the Chicago Wingate for seven months. The ladder was there, just waiting for her to keep climbing it.

Until this morning, anyway.

She had to get out of here. As things stood, her career was trashed and her life was in danger. If she could get out of this hotel room, she could at least take care of the latter problem. Or give herself a good running start anyway. Maybe she should just give him what he wanted. Would he let her go then? Surely he wouldn't want the added complication of having to kill someone needlessly cluttering up an otherwise harmless burglary? Then she remembered how swiftly and coolly he'd snapped those cords and tied her up. And there was that gun he happened to carry.

Then he was stepping out of the bathroom again. She hadn't thought it possible, but he was even better-looking dressed. He was wearing black slacks, nice leather shoes, a crisp white shirt that looked like it had been tailor made for his broad shoulders, and a tie in a muted pattern of black, forest green and gold. He'd combed his hair back off his face, leaving it to kick up and curl around the collar of his shirt.

As if reading her thoughts, he flashed a smile at her. "Back in a jiff."

She glared at him, but it seemed to have little impact as he strolled to the front hall and snagged a suit jacket from the closet. She didn't see the gun, which meant he was probably wearing it on his person. Nothing had been tucked in the back of his waistband. Ankle holster, she decided. Right before she decided she really needed to stop watching old detective shows on cable when she got up in the afternoon, before going on night shift.

She watched as he slid on his jacket, then took a slim black case from the nightstand and tucked it in an inside pocket. "Sit tight," he said, having the grace to look a little abashed as he said it, even with the twinkle still in his eyes.

She glared more fiercely and swore at him around the terry-cloth in her mouth, but he remained unfazed. Despite what he'd said, she'd half expected him to come over and take her key presently trapped between her hands. There was no way, short of head butting his solar plexus, that she could stop him. And that was only if he got really, really close. But, to her surprise, he left the room. The door shut behind him with a solid click. She craned her neck to see down the short hallway to the front door. Sure enough, the Do Not Disturb sign was gone. Any hope of a hotel maid rescue was gone.

It wasn't until she was truly alone that she began to panic in earnest. Which made no sense. He was gone, now was her time to focus. To channel her inner MacGyver and come up with a handy, homespun solution to getting out of this stupid chair and out of this room. The thing was, all those old detective shows had prop people to handily leave all the right items within reach.

She looked around, thinking if she could find anything that appeared sharp enough to cut through her bonds, she might be able to hop the chair in the direction, position herself accordingly and go to work. Except electrical cords were a lot harder to saw through than flimsy cotton rope.

Maybe if she tipped herself over onto her side, she could somehow get her fingers close enough to her ankle ties to loosen them up, but she then realized that changing position wouldn't really change the dynamics any. Which was why her degree was in hotel management, not physics. She tried bending forward far enough to see if she could get her teeth anywhere in the vicinity of her lap, but the moment she dipped down too far, the chair threatened to topple forward. Not a great idea since she had no way to protect herself from making a full face-plant. And fat lot of good that position would do her.

Then she remembered. He'd shaved his face. Which meant there was a razor in the bathroom somewhere. Maybe she could body hop the chair over to the bathroom. There was a small coffee table in the way, and she'd have to maneuver around the end of the bed, but it was worth a try.

It took her a few tries to do more than bobble the chair dangerously from one side to the other. The way he'd tied her feet, only her tippy toes touched the ground. Not much for leverage, but if she pushed and simultaneously lifted her butt off the seat, the chair did move a little. The only problem was she had no control over direction. Definitely looked a hell of a lot easier in the movies.

She tried not to get discouraged. She had no idea how long his idea of a "jiff" was, so she couldn't afford to waste any time. She bumped, leaned and bobbled until she'd managed to move the chair a whole two inches toward the end of the bed. Wonderful. She was sweating a little now, both from panic and exertion, which only served to make the electrical cords feel kind of icky. If only she sweat something helpful, like, say, olive oil, she might have been able to slip her wrists free. But no.

Then she had another thought. Slippery. He'd been in the shower, so maybe he used body soap. At the very least there'd be shampoo in there. Of course, she had no idea how she was going to retrieve these items while tied to a chair, but she wasn't going to sit there and do nothing. She'd figure that part out when she got in there.

Redoubling her efforts, she bobbled and scraped her way almost a whole foot, before the edge of the chair caught at the foot of the bed and went tottering all the way forward on two legs, before she swung the momentum back. The unfortunate result of that maneuver was that the chair overcorrected and tipped over backward, which she had no way of stopping. Thankfully the bed blocked the chair's descent, so she didn't whack her head on anything. But now she was tilted back like she was in some kind of recliner, with her feet completely off the floor, leaving her with no leverage at all.

MacGyver would be so disgusted with her right now. She was disgusted with her right now.

She carefully tried to shift her weight forward to see if she could tip it forward again, but that only served to make the back two chair legs—the only ones presently touching the floor—start to slip. She froze and tried to figure out what to do next.

Which was how Silas found her when he came back into the room. And did he honestly expect her to buy that as his name?

Although, maybe it was a popular name in New Zealand. She really didn't know.

He stood next to her, his head tipped sideways. "How on earth did you manage that position?" Then he smiled. "What are the odds of using that line with a woman in my own hotel room, and we're both fully clothed?"

She glared at him as fiercely as she was able. Her jaw was sore from having the stupid belt tucked in it, so she didn't bother trying to swear at him. She did wiggle a bit, but that proved to be a bad idea. The chair legs went out from under her, and it was only his amazingly swift reflexes that kept her from cracking her head on the floor.

He cradled the chair and gently tipped her upright. The whole time his body was in very close proximity to hers, which was why she couldn't help but notice how good he smelled. Not aftershave or cologne, not strong enough for that. Which meant shampoo. Or the body soap she'd been hoping to find earlier, when she'd started her ill-conceived mission. So much for channeling her inner MacGyver. More like her inner Lucy.

"You're a tenacious one. A shame we're on opposing sides." He moved around behind her. "I'm going to remove this, and while you might be tempted, I'll ask you not shout out, or right back on it goes."

She was so thankful to have the horrid thing off, she didn't do more than work her jaw once he'd removed the gag. "Thank you," she said, once he'd stepped around in front of her again and sat on the end of the bed. At least he had the decency to look slightly guilty. Of course, decency in a thief was highly overrated.

She wiggled her hands. "Can you untie me now?"

"I'm sorry," he said. "But there is too much at stake to take any chances with you."

"I wasn't tied up before you left and you managed to survive just fine."

He did smile a little at that, but it faded quickly. "We have to have a little talk."

She stilled. He looked...regretful. Had he decided she was too much trouble after all? The gun hadn't made a reappearance, so that was good news. But maybe he'd told someone about her misuse of the master passkey. Was someone on the way up to escort her from the hotel right this very second? "I'm sure we can come to some kind of mutually agreeable solution to this situation. Let's not do anything hasty."

"Oh, I believe I've found a solution to my problem. And perhaps, in the slightly longer term, yours as well. It seems I'm going to need a partner to help me complete my assignment here. If all goes well, we'll both get what we want."

4
_____

SHE DIDN'T LOOK NOTICEABLY upset or even put off by the proposal. Instead she wiggled her fingers. "I could help you break the law much better with my hands free."

"We'll get to that part." She looked adorably pathetic, but he refused to feel guilty. Sophie had, more or less, brought this on herself. She'd chosen a life of crime. Or at least a very early morning of it. He was merely going to extend her spree a wee bit.

She seemed to note that he still wasn't smiling, and sobered a bit herself. "What is it you want me to do? Am I going from trashing my career to risking serious jail time?"

"You haven't trashed anything. Yet. Help me get what I want, I return home, you go back to work. You'll have done a good deed, and for that, no one will ever be the wiser about your early morning breaking and entering."

"I entered, I didn't break. I had a key. And that was also an attempt at doing a good deed, and look where that landed me?" But her attempt at bravado was short-lived, as, a moment later, her expression faltered causing her to look down at her still-tied hands.

On anyone else, he'd have suspected it to be a calculated ploy of some sort, but he already knew that to be beyond her.

"What is it?" he asked. When she didn't look up, he said, "Sophie?"

She took another moment, then sighed and looked at him. "I realize this means nothing to you, it's just, I'm worried. About Delia. That's my friend, whose phone I was trying to retrieve. There's a better than average chance that all hell is breaking loose right about now."

He couldn't take his eyes off her. She'd been fascinating before, with her so-innocent eyes and nervous babble. But she was truly something when her heart was in play, as it clearly was where her friend was concerned. And, she was right, he didn't—couldn't—care about that. The only good that knowledge did him was provide him with possible leverage to get what he wanted. This Delia was a weakness to be exploited. Nothing more.

Now it was his turn to look away, away from those beseeching eyes of hers. He couldn't let himself care, he knew that… but that didn't mean he was particularly fond of himself at that moment. "If your friend is as toxic as you've made her seem, perhaps it will be a good thing you're not to be found then. For both of your sakes."

Her eyes narrowed. "Meaning what, exactly?"

"Meaning you'll be mercifully removed from having to do God knows what to rescue your friend, and she'll be forced to handle her own problems. Might not be a bad thing for her to deal with the consequences of her actions."

"Yes, well, given I'm not exactly loving being schooled on that particular lesson myself at the moment, it'd be a bit hypocritical to wish it on my best friend. And I told you, her fiancé is Adam Wingate. The wedding reception will be held here this coming weekend and—"

"I thought you also said that you weren't invited."

"What I'm saying is that the hotel is going to be crawling with all kinds of extra people and security, planning, setting up and in general getting ready for what will be a major media event, at least here in town."

He frowned. Bugger. That could complicate things. "We can work around that. In fact, maybe we can use the general frenzy to our advantage."

Now she frowned. "How? You already know I'm a lousy liar, so having me try to pretend that nothing is going on is going to be hard enough, much less pretending around my best friend and my coworkers. And I can't exactly sneak around in my own hotel and not be noticed."

"I don't need you to be noticed."

"You said accomplice."

"I said partner. A…covert partnership."

"Covert." She narrowed her eyes. "I know you caught me sneaking in here, but if you think I'm going to sneak into some man's room and… You know, I thought I made it clear before that I wasn't—"

His brows lifted a bit at her meaning. "Trust me, that's the last thing I'd ask of you." He frowned when she looked insulted.

"Is it so impossible to believe that I could seduce someone?"

What? His attention was all caught up in her eyes. So expressive, so direct. So at odds with the sweet, innocent face and those oh-so-soft-looking lips. It was their collective impact that had him speaking before he could think better of it. "Oh, I think you have weapons and wiles you're not even aware of, which makes you particularly dangerous."

Her lips parted at that, and he watched her pupils expand. It made parts of him expand a little, too. How was it they went from sparring to…this, he had no idea, but he had to regain control over whatever it was she seemed to so effortlessly do to him, and keep his focus on the prize.

Which was the Shay emerald…not Sophie Maplethorpe. And yet, in her own way, Sophie sparkled far brighter than that priceless heirloom he was trying to re-retrieve. Whether vulnerable or irritated, there was always a spark of vitality in her eyes. It struck him as truly remarkable that she'd come all this way in life, and didn't seem to have the slightest grasp of where her powers truly lay. But that's what made her so intoxicating.

"Thank you. I think."

"It was a compliment," he assured her, trying not to shift to find a more comfortable fit to his trousers. "Though perhaps one better kept to myself."

She looked at him then, truly looked at him. As if seeing something in him she hadn't seen before.

"What?" he asked, warily knowing he shouldn't.

"In my field, it pays to be a good reader of people."

"And?"

She tilted her head just slightly. "While, on the surface, it might be quite plausible that you're some kind of international criminal, a closer look tells me that you're no ruthless thief."

"I've threatened you with a gun, bound and gagged you."

"You have kind eyes."

He should have laughed at that. Outright. Instead he found himself simply looking at her. Perhaps into her. So innocent, and yet, not really. Not when it came to knowing things that others never took the time to notice. Dangerously innocent, his Sophie Maplethorpe.

"Ruthless thieves are supposed to have soulless eyes. Yours are warm, and they crinkle at the corners. You smile often." She smiled a little herself at that. "Ruthless thieves probably don't."

He didn't know what he'd been expecting her to say, but it wasn't that, and her simply stated assessment took him somewhat aback. He felt oddly exposed. "I'm sure there are plenty of thieves, ruthless and otherwise, who can fake all kinds of appearances."

"You're probably right. You were quite…efficient with those electrical cords." She sighed, just a little, but the co-inciding tug it elicited inside him had him straightening and striding across the room.

He needed some space between them. Moreso, he needed to get his equilibrium back, and swiftly. "So—"

"Still," she interrupted, "I was thinking that maybe you should just tell me why you're here. You already know I'm a sucker for a sob story, or I wouldn't have been in your room in the first place. Maybe I'll want to help you, blackmail not required."

"You think I came here for a kindly reason, then, is that it? A mission to match the eyes, as it were."

She lifted her shoulder, then winced when it tugged at the cord on her wrists. So, in addition to becoming a thief, he was officially a cad of the first order. He could honestly say that this was his first time tying up a woman in his hotel room—for any reason—and it wasn't a proud moment, seeing her there, like that.

"Have you ever used your gun?"

"What?" If she'd simply be consistent for more than five minutes, maybe he'd get a handle on this situation, on her, but she was dashedly quixotic. "I believe I did, earlier."

"I don't mean waving it around. Have you ever shot… anything?"

"I wasn't waving it about, I was aiming it. At you."

She shivered. "Yes, I haven't forgotten that part. But that's not what I asked."

"If you're trying to insinuate that because I haven't shot at anything, that I'm somehow a kinder, gentler thief—"

"Recovery specialist," she corrected him, the barest hint of mockery in her voice.

"The use of a firearm is hardly an accurate measure of the man wielding it. And why in bloody hell are we having this conversation?" He stalked to the other corner of the room, opened the bar fridge, then realized it was far too early in the day for a drink, and slapped it shut again. "We have business to attend. No more tomfoolery."

"No, we wouldn't want any more of that."

He raked a hand through his hair, swore under his breath, then walked back to the bed and forced himself to sit calmly on the edge, his knees inches now from hers. How was it she could so frustrate him…and yet all he could think, even now, when he looked at her, was how she'd look bound to the bedposts instead of that chair. Writhing, those too-soft curves of hers, straining against—"We need to discuss the plan," he said, abruptly.

"The plan," she repeated, unfazed by his harsh tone.

"The…recovery plan."

"Ah."

He lifted an eyebrow. "I didn't throw the gun away, you know."

"I doubted I'd be that lucky."

He wanted nothing more than to kiss that too-knowing look right off her face. Would serve her right, possibly even shock her into some much needed silence. Her feminine wiles seemed to be the only weapon she didn't realize she had.

So, why on earth he thought he should be the one to introduce her to them, he had no idea. But now that the seed was planted in his brain…and a few other parts of his anatomy…he couldn't seem to ignore it. "Your key card," he all but blurted. *Focus, Lassiter. Focus.* "What are the boundaries of use? Is there any record of where it's been used?"

"Only if the scanner it's used in is screened. The card itself doesn't have that feature. Where do you want me to use it?"

"Not you, me. I need you for other things."

There went her pupils again, and dammit if she didn't take a quick look at the bed.

"You—" She stopped, cleared her throat. "Such as?"

"As you said, trotting about might draw undue attention

from folks we'd rather not be drawing attention from. What I need from you is information on how the security system works. Then I'll be borrowing your card for a bit, and—"

"But, you made it sound, before, like you wanted me to do something other than just give you insider information."

Simon briefly closed his eyes. He felt naked with her in a way he never did. With anyone. Maybe he should just get her naked and keep her off balance like she was keeping him. "I had a thought, when I came in earlier, that perhaps things would go more swiftly if you did, indeed, accompany me on a small part of my assignment here, but you've since convinced me that would be unwise."

"Because I'm frustrating and lousy at lying?"

"Partly, yes," he said honestly, and found himself fighting a smile when she scowled, even though they both knew it was true. "And because, as you so helpfully pointed out, you're too closely connected to a major media event being staged here. I've decided not to risk that."

"Well, I suppose if you have my key card, you won't have to risk much of anything, except getting caught."

"All the more reason to leave you tied up. If I'm found out and they go hunting, they'll find you here, an obvious victim of a crime."

"Why should I believe for even a second that you'd tell them anything except what would help save your hide?"

He gave in to the urge then, and smiled. "Kind eyes?"

A short laugh spluttered out before she could catch it. It was surprisingly rich, what little taste he got of it—he would have expected something lighter, more lilting. But then, Sophie was turning out to be anything but the expected.

The moment extended…and expanded. Both of them smiling, looking at each other…into each other. He wasn't sure who leaned closer first. The pull to her was powerfully strong, like the positive and negative ends of two magnets, inexorably drawn toward one another by a force seemingly bigger than each alone could ever produce. And he thought, in that moment where everything slowed down, that if he could just get a taste of her, feel her move and breathe, warm and alive beneath his touch, that he'd have a better sense of how to handle her.

And he knew, even as he thought it, that it was a lie even he couldn't sell himself. He wanted all of those things, almost more than he wanted his next breath, and it had nothing whatsoever to do with finding leverage or gaining the advantage.

He'd taken the Shay emerald from Guinn MacRanald and given it to Langston Tolliver, thinking the latter to be the rightful owner, as his extensive documentation would lead any sane man to believe. Only now he knew, as his gut had instructed him all along, that he'd taken the stone from its true owner, robbing Guinn of his rightful heritage and the one thing that symbolized all that the MacRanald ancestry was…a heritage he hadn't realized that Tolliver would do anything to destroy. He should have done his research, should have at least followed his gut that far…but hadn't thought it necessary, with the documents before him.

Only to find those niggling suspicions had been right all along, and he'd been the victim of a very cleverly mounted con.

He was here to fix that, to right that. Not to get involved with a saucy, innocent, electrifyingly compelling American who would do nothing but lead him down a path of total distraction…and, ultimately, destruction. Tolliver was here in Chicago to boast of his triumphant recovery of the stone to the world at large…and to Guinn in particular. After which, Simon was absolutely certain it would be secreted away, never to be seen in public again…certainly far out of even Simon's capable reach.

That was all he should be concerning himself with. Even a quick toss in the sheets had to be off-limits.

Besides which, he already knew that Sophie Maplethorpe was hardly the dallying kind. And a more unlikely beginning to any other sort of a relationship there could never be. If he was a man who wanted that kind of thing. Which...he wasn't.

At the last possible second, with her breath on his lips, he groaned and pushed away from the bed, stalking to the window where she couldn't spy just how fiercely aroused he was. He stared out the window but saw nothing, as he contemplated telling her the truth about why he was here. She had *heroine* stamped all over her.

But even though she might have bent the rules by breaking into his room to help a friend, he'd bet money she would have a hard time living with herself if she was made to do something truly against principal. She'd talk herself into it, whether it was because she believed in it, or because she wanted to preserve her career, her good name, whatever...but afterward, she'd wrestle with it, lose sleep over it, and eventually end up going to her superiors and regretfully informing them of her actions. Even if it cost her everything.

He knew this because he was here, risking everything, for the same reasons.

Only he wasn't leaving here without what he came for. So lines would be crossed at some point. Which meant the risk had already been taken. She might not know much, but she already knew enough.

He paced. She remained silent. It was rather unnerving, really. How she alternated between nervous babbling one moment, and absolute quiet the next. It was almost as if she knew him. As if she knew letting him stew and think things through would eventually get her what she wanted.

He finally sat down on the edge of the bed again. "Okay. Here's the thing."

Her soft gray eyes went on full alert. Her china doll lips pursed in anticipation.

And, dammit to hell, he really, really had to find a way to

stop noticing both of those things. "There is something here, in this hotel, that rightfully belongs to someone else."

"What sort of thing is it?"

"That's not important."

"It is if I'm going to help you get it back."

"Sophie—"

"Fine," she said, then looked at him with that intent gaze again. "Are you sure you're as good at this as you think you are?"

His eyes narrowed at the taunt. "I'm quite good at what I do," he said flatly. "And that is due partly, if not wholly, to the fact that I rely only on myself to get the job done. I shouldn't have to point out which one of us is currently tied to a chair."

"How about you untie me, and I promise I won't scream or try anything foolish while we talk about what I'm helping you steal back over breakfast?"

He scooped up the bathrobe belt and she immediately looked nervous.

"Okay, okay, so you don't have to feed me."

"Trade-off," he said. "I'll untie you, but then this has to go on. At least until after the food is delivered."

She seemed to consider that for a moment. "I can't persuade you to trust me?"

"No more than you would trust me if the situation were reversed."

"I'd like to think I'd be this hard-core about things, but I know myself too well."

"Which is why you're not a thief."

"And you are?"

He walked around behind her and crouched down. "You know, I'm beginning to think the gag might be a good idea for a couple of reasons."

"Very funny," she said, then averted her head when he tried to tie it on. "Silas, please."

He paused because of the earnestness in her voice. And because it felt wrong, somehow, not hearing his real name on her lips.

So much for being hard-core.

He stood and tossed the belt on the bed as he walked to the nightstand phone.

"Thank you," she said, as quietly as he'd ever heard her.

"Don't thank me yet," he muttered, and snatched the phone off the hook.

5

SOPHIE DIDN'T SCREAM and for that, she got scrambled eggs, a croissant, freshly squeezed orange juice and the use of her hands. She wasn't sure what it said about her that she felt like this was major progress. Or that she was able to eat at all, much less inhale the food on her plate like a half-starved supermodel the day after retirement. It was the closest she'd ever come to feeling like a supermodel, retired or otherwise, so she tried to embrace the moment.

And ignore the man sitting across the table from her.

Neither worked, really.

Of course, there was that moment by the bed. And it was a moment. She was sure of it. The way he'd looked at her, like a man who wanted…things. Possibly, her. And she'd wanted. In that moment, she'd wanted. Okay, so there had been a lot of wanting moments in the time since she'd flung panties in his face. Which seemed a lifetime ago now. But he'd leaned. And for a brief, heart-stopping second, she'd been certain he was going to kiss her. And she'd wanted that, too.

Still did, if she were being painfully honest with herself.

"So," she said, shoving away those very foolish thoughts, trying to look completely cool and collected. But mostly trying not to choke on the pulp in her orange juice as she took a sip to clear the sudden tightness that gripped her throat every time she looked at him and remembered "the moment." She coughed and took a renewed interest in her eggs. "You were going to tell me about your occupation."

"Was I?"

She braved a glance at him, before the eggs lured her back. Whoever thought of putting cheese and cream in scrambled eggs should be canonized, she thought, as she scooped up another heaping forkful. Had she ever been this ravenous? Why was she so ravenous? Nerves usually made her nauseous. "Yes," she said, around another bite, "you were. How does a person get started in the field of...recovering things?"

"You mean did I start my life as Oliver Twist, picking pockets and running scams, then find some way to romantically turn those ill-gotten skills into a legally responsible profession, at which I went on to shine like the brightest star and am now, sitting here before you, a humble, yet noble hero, champion of the poor and downtrodden?"

She paused with the fork halfway to her mouth and stared at him. "Wow." She took the bite, thought for a moment, chewed, swallowed, then nodded. "Yeah, pretty much."

"That's exactly how I got started."

She wrestled with the tiny lid to the jar of blackberry preserves.

He reached over and plucked the jar from her hands, and she was so momentarily stunned by the warmth of his skin brushing hers, the blunt feel of his fingers, that her brain sort of short-circuited for an instant, her senses all reveling in that brief contact.

He popped the lid and handed the jar to her and turned his attention back to the omelet he was very precisely cutting pieces from, and thoughtfully chewing, in between sips of tea—yes, tea—and reading the morning paper.

To anyone else it might look as if they were a longtime couple going through their morning ritual. Of course, if anyone else were looking, they might also wonder why her ankles were tied to the chair, but, all things considered, it was a minor aberration to an otherwise quaint domestic scene.

"Have you ever been arrested?" she asked him as she polished off the last of the croissant, wishing she had another.

"You mean during my long life of crime?" He folded the paper and laid it beside his plate. "No, I've managed to avoid getting thrown in the slammer, as you Yanks call it."

"Good to know," she said, reluctantly putting her silverware on her plate, still hungry. She'd heard that being put in sudden danger could amp up all kinds of emotions in people, like making them want to have sex with someone they would otherwise never consider getting naked with. Maybe for her, it was exhibiting itself as hunger. She looked at Silas. Nope, it was sex for her, too. Except she was pretty sure it wouldn't have taken a crisis situation to make her want him.

He looked up then, and caught her staring…only he didn't look away. He didn't say a word, and she couldn't have if she'd wanted to; her throat had completely closed over. He kept his gaze on hers until her thighs were all kind of quivery and her skin felt tingly, and all she could do was think about how warm his skin had felt, and that the bluntness of his fingertips had been so incredibly….male. And how they might feel playing out on other parts of her body. She jerked her gaze away, and would have gotten up from the table to put some much needed distance between them, but realized quite quickly that she couldn't go anywhere.

His expression flickered, and for just a split second, it was like the moment all over again. The way he looked at her, like he was the one with the ravenous appetite. It made her want to squirm, when it should have downright terrified her. She was tied to a chair for God's sake. The last person she should be lusting after was the man who'd put her there.

Just then the phone rang, making her jump.

The moment mercifully ended, she took a deep, steadying

breath as Silas shoved his chair back and went to answer it. She craned her neck, almost tipping the chair sideways, in hopes of getting at least a hint of who was on the other end. No matter how hard she listened, though, she heard nothing. He barely spoke a word. Everything else that was going on rushed back through her mind. She tried not to think about what was happening with Delia at that very moment. Or if anyone had missed her yet. Of course, pretty much everyone else in her orbit would assume she was at home sleeping. Oh, if only. She put her napkin on the table and took a steadying breath. She needed to stop thinking about wanting Silas to put his hands on her again, and formulate an exit plan.

She glanced at the bed, but quickly looked away. No naked thoughts! Seducing him probably wouldn't have worked anyway. It was highly likely he slept with actual supermodels.

He hung up the phone and then it hit her. *Idiot!* He'd been standing far from the door with his back to her and she'd had perfectly free hands to untie her ankles! Well, the knots were behind her, but surely she'd have been able to do something. Saw through the cables with her jam knife, something. Instead she'd sat there like a sex-starved dork—which, okay, so there might be some truth to that. She sighed as Silas crossed back to the table, and mentally added thief and spy to the list of things she'd suck at doing, right after supermodel.

He didn't look all that happy as he took his seat across from her. Now that breakfast was over, would he tie her up again? That would significantly reduce her possible exit strategies.

"So, the good news is I won't need your help getting into the hotel safe."

She blanched. Up until then, even with the gun and tying her up, it had all seemed somewhat surreal. But now there was talk of safe-cracking and actual plans being made and it felt a lot more real. And she was suddenly a lot less hungry and a lot more nauseous. "Good to know," she managed. "It would be next to impossible for me to take anything from there anyway, given how it's set up. I—I thought you needed to get into another room."

"I wasn't a hundred percent sure where it was."

"But you are now."

"Close enough. I'm still going to need that passkey of yours."

"Okay."

"Okay?"

"I've decided I can't be a party to whatever else it is you're doing, even if it is for a good cause. I mean, it's bad enough, yes, that I broke in here, and I apologized for that. So, it's my fault if my passkey gets stolen and used inappropriately. To steal God only knows what." She flung up her hand. "Which I do not want to know! I've changed my mind about having to know things. Just take it already and do whatever you have to do. I want to go home, get some sleep, find out if my best friend's life is over, then go back to work."

Silas looked at her so intently her thighs went all tingly again. "I wish it were that simple."

"It is that simple. I will take the blame for losing my passkey and I might lose my job over that alone, especially as it will be tied to a robbery. So you've got nothing really over me. That's the worst that can happen. Right?" She looked at him. "Never mind, I don't want to know that, either. I would be horrible in jail, really I would. I wouldn't fare well."

He smiled then. "You might do better than you think. But if all goes as planned, there won't be jail time in either of our futures."

She thought she'd had a clearer mind, but maybe that was the sugar rush from all that jam talking. That apparently had subsided now, because she was both very scared and very tired. "Well, that's certainly a relief."

"I'm sorry, but I also need your help. Personally."

"Just take the damn key," she said, already trying to figure out how she could be as inconspicuous as possible in prison.

They didn't target the quiet ones, did they? Why hadn't she watched more prison chick movies? She had no idea what to expect.

"Sophie." He'd said it gently, and she was looking up, responding, before thinking better of it.

"What?"

"I need you to break into the room. I can't go in there."

"Why? Why can't you go?"

"I can't be seen entering or exiting that room. You'll have to be quiet when you go in," he went on, as if it were decided already.

"Who cares about how quiet I am? It's not like there's going to be anyone—" She broke off and her mouth dropped open for a second, before snapping back shut. "No. No way. You know firsthand that I don't do well sneaking around in occupied rooms."

"You can pretend you're the maid. I'm sure we can get the right gear for that."

She started to spout right back at him, until she realized that he was talking about her moving about the hotel, getting uniforms, which meant going to other floors, other areas. Where there were people. Even if he went with her every step of the way, there would have to be moments where she could break free. It was risky, but sitting here tied up wasn't going to get her anywhere except in jail. Or worse.

"We could, but why not just wait for whoever is in there to leave, then go in yourself?"

"It won't be there unless the room is occupied."

"Oh." She frowned. "What is it, exactly, that you're stealing back?" She held up a hand. "I'm sorry, re-retrieving?"

"I won't need your help until this evening," he said, ignoring her question. "I won't be needing the bed and I know you worked all last night, so it's yours. For now."

"I have to work this evening," she said, trying not to care

that he seemed entirely unmoved, much less tempted, by her being in his bed.

"You'll have to ask for the night off." He raised his hand as she opened her mouth. "If I could make this happen earlier and set us both free, trust me, I would."

She clamped her lips together. Great. Not only wasn't he tempted by her in any physical way, he couldn't get rid of her fast enough. Clearly she'd misread that moment earlier. Not that this wasn't a good thing in the big scheme of things, but it was kind of insulting.

"It's all going to be over by tonight," he said. "We'll both get what we want, and never have to see each other again."

"What, exactly, do you want me to do? Because, as it stands, you have me for breaking and entering, and now it sounds like you want me to do the actual stealing—"

"Retrieving," he said.

"Right. I'm sure the police will be mollified by that distinction when they haul me in. Anyway, if I retrieve whatever it is for you, then basically I'm the one who is screwed and you, pretty much, haven't done anything wrong."

The corner of his mouth quirked. "Funny how that works out, eh?"

"Funny how I'm not really all that amused." A totally hot accent only went so far. Okay, it went pretty far, but this was too far.

"If I could do this any other way, I would. If it makes you feel any better, I can assure you that you are doing a good thing, a favor, if you will, for someone completely deserving, and I'm not speaking of myself here."

"So, why won't you tell me what's going on, then? I mean, if it's a good deed—"

"I believe you said you didn't want any additional information."

"That was before I found out I was the one doing the stealing."

"Re—"

"—trieving. Okay." She sighed. "You're going to have to tell me at least part of it, or I won't know what to *retrieve*." She made finger quotes in the air with that last part, which didn't seem to amuse him. Too bad.

"It's an old—very old—velvet case. You don't need to know more than that. I am trying to keep you from being any more involved than necessary."

"Right. I feel very cared-for in this scenario."

"Sophie—"

He really had to stop saying her name. It sounded way too good the way he said it. "What's to keep me from just taking it myself? Or telling whoever is in that room that you're making me steal against my will?"

Any vestiges of a smile or amusement vanished completely. "You cannot do that."

"Well, I could, but if you tell me what I'm doing this for, or who—"

"It would only put you in real trouble."

"As opposed to the fake trouble I'm in now?"

He leaned his weight onto the table, bringing his face closer and his gaze that much more intently focused on her. It wasn't anything like the last time they'd leaned. This time it scared her a little. More than a little. Which, she suspected, it was supposed to.

"My goal is to get what I came for and set you free, unharmed, to go back to the life you were living before I met you. The person in that room will not be similarly motivated. And is also far more equipped to cause harm, and not nearly as reluctant to do so. Of that, I assure you."

Yep, she was officially scared.

6

SIMON'S HEART HAD SQUEEZED like someone had it in their fist at the thought of Sophie being cavalier around Tolliver. He told himself it was because he didn't want anyone getting hurt, but looking at Sophie, he had to at least admit that there might be more at play there. She…did something to him. Made him care. Certainly more than he should. She also made him want. If he caught her looking at him like she had that jam-laden croissant, then looking at the bed, one more time, he might not be responsible for his actions.

Bloody hell. He had to stop wrestling with his conscience—and his hormones—and get them both focused on the matter at hand. He'd gone down to the lobby earlier and done his best to charm the youngest, most inexperienced front-desk registrar into inadvertently revealing whether or not Tolliver had checked anything into the hotel safe.

Behaving as if he was an acquaintance of the old Brit, which, in point of fact, he was, Simon had joked with her about whether or not they would have space for the important objets d' art he planned to purchase while in town, or if Tolliver's crates containing the collection he was donating to the Art Institute for the gala that weekend had taken up all the room. She'd blushingly assured him that they could handle whatever he brought in and added that, as far as she knew, Tolliver's crates must not have arrived as he hadn't checked anything into the safe.

Of course, Tolliver's crates would have gone directly to the museum, but the desk help didn't know that. Mission accomplished.

Which meant the Shay was wherever Tolliver was. Which was unfortunate, but not surprising. He was a control freak who didn't trust a soul. And he wasn't in his room, which was what the phone call just now had informed him of. This significantly reduced his chances at retrieving the Shay. If Tolliver spotted him, he'd know exactly why Simon was there.

But now he had Sophie. And Tolliver wouldn't suspect her of anything.

"So, this old velvet case you're retrieving, it's a favor for a friend? And the person you're taking it from doesn't play well with others. Does your friend know what kind of trouble this could land you in?"

"No more so, I'd venture to say, than your friend did when she asked you for help."

Sophie opened her mouth, then shut it again and gave him a rueful look. "Given my success rate thus far, I'm surprised you're willing to trust me with this."

"My options are limited." Which was exceedingly true. Not knowing what exactly Tolliver had in mind by coming to the States and being the benefactor behind the art gala exhibit, Simon hadn't been able to put any specific plan in place. He'd only known that Tolliver never did anything, certainly not splashy as this, given he was otherwise a man who enjoyed his privacy, without there being an ulterior motive. And when he'd tracked him and the Shay to Heathrow, he'd known even as he'd boarded the flight that it had something to do with his vendetta against Guinn MacRanald. Tolliver had won, but he hadn't finished destroying Guinn completely. It wouldn't be enough just to have the Shay in his possession. No, Tolliver would want to make certain that Guinn knew exactly what he'd done, while the world watched.

The gala event was Friday evening, likely the only time the Shay would be on display. And given the person who'd checked in with Tolliver, Simon had a pretty good idea of exactly how he intended to display it.

If he didn't snag it from Tolliver's room before then, then the only other window of opportunity would be taking it directly off the neck of Tolliver's roommate. He had a name now, but hadn't had the time, given his unexpected guest, to look her up. Just because he didn't recognize it, didn't mean anything. He didn't exactly spend time keeping up with the glitterati. But, likely as not, she was a model or starlet of some reknown who would showcase the emerald around a slender neck, topped by a high-wattage smile, and, most importantly, plenty of media coverage every time she so much as batted a lash.

In Tolliver's mind, there would be no better way to make an international statement of ownership than to have the piece on his arm, as it were, highly visible for all to see. But Simon knew he was insanely possessive of his assets, most especially this one, and that the Shay would be vaulted immediately upon his return to London.

And Tolliver's safe didn't have a convenient passkey.

"So, I'm basically a desperation move," Sophie said. "There's a hearty endorsement. I feel much better about this now."

Now he sighed. "Listen, I don't like this any more than you do."

"I might like it even less."

"Let's call it a draw. The bottom line is, I need to retrieve something from a fellow guest that does not belong to him, and return it to its rightful owner. My best chance of doing that is here and now. However, I'm known to your guest, and, let's just say—"

"He wouldn't be all that excited to see you?"

"An understatement."

"Ah."

"Indeed."

"So why not wait for this guest to leave his room, and then do…whatever it is you do?"

"Because it goes where he goes."

"Oh." Her shoulders lost a bit of their rigidness. "So, he carries this thing with him?"

"Yes. Or his companion might."

"There are *two* people in the room? Silas—"

"Simon."

She blinked. "What?"

He swore under his breath. A fine thief he made. "It's Simon. Lassiter. There, now you have leverage. More than I should be giving if I knew what was good for me, but if that were the case, I wouldn't be here, now would I? No, I'd be back in London, working a normal assignment like a regular, sane bloke who hasn't managed to bungle things up and land himself in this ridiculous situation." He ended with another string of epithets.

She waited a beat to make sure he was finished, then smiled. "Impressive. Are you like this all the time when you're stressed? Or am I rubbing off on you?"

"I wouldn't hazard to guess at this point."

"Well, thank you. Simon." She tilted her head slightly. "It suits you, you know."

"My mum, God rest her soul, would thank you for that. She fought my father on that score. It's an old family name on her side."

"What did your father want to name you?"

"Bartholomew. After himself."

She made a face. "I'm glad your mom stuck to her guns. No insult to your dad, of course. But that's a lot to saddle a kid with."

"They compromised."

She eyed him. "You have siblings, then? Your poor younger brother got it instead?"

He shook his head. It took her a moment, then she laughed. "Simon Bartholomew Lassiter?"

"In the flesh."

Her cheeks suddenly flushed a bit. "Mmm" was all she said, then swiftly went on. "Sounds like they had a good relationship. Compromising, I mean. Not everyone is good at that. And I'm sorry she's no longer with you. Your eyes warm up a lot when you talk about her."

Her expression took on an empathy he didn't usually see when that information popped up. Which it rarely did as he wasn't in the habit of discussing his family with anyone. But on the rare occasion that he did, the reaction was usually one of pity. He had no use for that, but this was...effective.

"I lost my mother, too," she said. "When I was nine. And my father. Car accident. Icy roads. My grandmother raised me. She passed five years ago."

He dipped his chin then, breaking eye contact. They shouldn't be doing this. This...getting to know about each other thing. It was bad enough he'd drawn her into this, bad enough he was drawn to her, period. And he was. Drawn. And the tugging was getting stronger. "I'm sorry to hear that," he said, intending to sound sincere, but in a way that didn't brook further conversation. Only it didn't accomplish that at all. Probably because he truly was sincere.

"Brain aneurysm," Sophie said, both bluntly and a bit wistfully. How she managed that, he didn't know. "My grandmother, I mean. She was gone in a blink."

"Very sorry," he said, and meant it.

She didn't say more, and he felt the weight of her expectation that he return the gesture of faith by sharing his own tale. "We need to discuss strategy," he said. "I don't want to unnecessarily compromise you, but—"

"Simon."

He should have never told her his name. He'd hated hearing her call him something false, but this was almost worse. Far worse, actually. "Nothing so dramatic, I assure you," he said, by way of explanation. When he looked up to find her watching him expectantly, and with exaggerated patience, he sighed and said, "Complications during surgery. She'd had a kidney transplant and there were continuing problems. She hadn't been in such good shape before, so it was sad, but not entirely unexpected."

"How long ago?"

"I'd just completed university. Eight years, I suppose it is now."

"Was she…what did you call yourself? Kiwi?"

He shook his head. "Aussie, part Malaysian. Born in Melbourne. Her parents moved to the North Island when she was seventeen. My father, as his father before him, was a vintner in Hawke's Bay. They met when her parents were looking for work in the area. He thought she was the most beautiful thing he'd ever seen and forever treated her as such."

"That's…so lovely," Sophie said, sounding surprised. She blinked her eyes a couple of times and looked down at her hands for a moment. "She sounds like a very lucky woman, despite the physical setbacks. A husband who adored her and a son—"

"Who is forcing a complete stranger to steal for him. Yes, she'd be ever so proud."

Sophie surprised him by smiling at that. "I wouldn't say complete strangers." The smile softened. "Not now."

He looked at her then, truly looked at her, and found himself shaking his head.

"What?" she said, no longer smiling. "What have I done or said now? If you're worried that sharing details of your life with me is somehow weakening your position, I can assure you, you're quite wrong on that."

"I'm getting that."

"Are you? Then why the look? As if I'm ridiculous some-how."

Funny, he thought, how she turned all kinds of pink when thinking of his person, his body, but had no problem chal-lenging him intellectually, debating him to his face. "Hardly that. Far from that. I just… You just sort of barge ahead, you know, into life. You're bright and intelligent, but sometimes your common sense—"

"I realize that given my current position, I can hardly de-bate the merits of my wits or lack thereof, but I assure you, I didn't get to be manager of this place before turning thirty because I'm a bubblehead."

He started to rebut, then stopped. Then laughed. Then shook his head again. "No, you're no bubblehead."

"Thank you."

"You're quite welcome." He thought about trying to explain to her what it was about her that was such an enigma to him, but decided he hadn't quite figured that out himself just yet, so best to leave this conversation be entirely for the moment. Forever, if he was smart. But his wits could hardly be called sharp since she'd come into his life, either.

"I do barge ahead, as you put it," she said, after the silence had spun out a few moments longer than necessary. "But I feel like life demands that. If you want to get anywhere, you're not going to do it sitting around and waiting, you know? I know I don't look like some fierce boardroom warrior woman, but I can hardly do anything about the face I was handed, much less the rest." She gestured to her body, which he was trying—fiercely—to cease responding to, and mostly failing. He was having even less luck not thinking about it.

Along with those deluxe lips and fistfuls of soft curls, she had an ample figure. *Ample.* That was the word. Bordering on voluptuous. *Lush.* A word he'd never used once, and yet she was it, personified. She was softly rounded in all the right places. No bony shoulders or stringy arms. No jutting hips or stalklike legs. Her hips flared broadly, and though he could probably span her waist with his hands, if he cupped them over her breasts, he was certain he couldn't contain their fullness in his palms. She was wearing rather sexless trousers, but he'd bet her legs were shapely and strong from all the walking and running around this place that she must do as part of her job. He knew from personal observation when she'd been bent over, digging in that chair, that there were no trousers sexless enough to hide her heartshaped backside.

Yeah, the last thing he needed was her referring to her face or her body. She might not look like a warrior woman, but she'd most certainly laid siege to him like one.

"But just because I look like some naive milkmaid from an eighteenth-century British painting, doesn't mean I think like one."

He wanted to beg her to stop handing him more imagery to torture himself with. "You have this rose-colored-glasses sort of permanent optimism about you. Which is a great attitude, but there is a guilelessness to it that…well, I'd think, especially in a city this big, in this kind of environment, that you'd have long since been chewed up whole, or had the rosy stomped out of you."

"Have you?"

He laughed then, but there was no humor in it. "I don't know that my temperament or outlook on life would ever have been described as *rosy*."

"Your parents sound like they were pretty rosy, so it only goes to follow you would've at least observed it growing up. I have no idea what's happened to make you change your mind about it, but I think we all do the best with what we have, or at least try to. That's a rosy outlook. And, despite setbacks to that natural optimism, I've fared okay. Until this morning, anyway."

"I suppose you have," he said, somewhat thoughtfully.

"But you think you haven't? Hard to believe two people who loved like you say they did would raise a son who didn't believe in it."

"I didn't say I didn't believe in love or the kind of commitment my parents shared."

"Well, if you believe in that, then you're an optimist."

"That doesn't make any sense. You can believe in the power of love, even if you're cynical enough to question people's motives. Not everyone is loving and kind—"

"Nor is everyone sinister and mean."

"Exactly."

"And it takes an optimist to know the difference. A pessimist would assume the worst. Clearly, you don't. Or you wouldn't be here risking what you're risking for the sake of a friend."

"There are all kinds of motives for doing the right thing. Don't be so swift to ascribe heroic qualities to me. I'm here to do the right thing, but only because I did the wrong thing first. A very wrong thing."

She laughed.

He frowned. "You find that amusing?"

"No. I find it human." She gestured to her currently bound ankles. "I know all about being human. And occasionally doing very wrong things." He started to respond, but she held up her hand. "Just tell me one thing. When you were doing that very wrong thing, did you know it was wrong? What I mean, I guess, is were you intentionally causing harm to someone?"

"I thought I was helping," he said, very honestly. "But I should have questioned what I thought I knew. I had enough clues to the contrary."

She shrugged. "Human."

He sighed and rolled his suddenly weary shoulders. "We have a small window, and a lot to discuss."

"We're going to be spending the next who-knows-how-many hours together, right? Trust building isn't a bad thing."

"Sophie—"

She lifted her hands, palms out, in surrender. "So, when do I start my new life as a cat burglar?"

"Excuse me?"

"Sounds more exciting than common thief. Well, unless it's being a jewel thief. That's always been a more—" She broke off, as if she'd noted some change in his expression.

Which was unfortunate, as he'd been really careful not to have one. But then, around her it was hard to maintain anything for any length of time since he never knew what was going to come out of her mouth next.

"I'm stealing jewelry? Seriously? As in really, ridiculously expensive jewelry? Of course, what other kind would you steal, right? And if it's in an old velvet case, I'm guessing really, really old, expensive jewelry."

"What's in the case isn't important."

"Of course it's important. Stealing heirloom gemstones isn't like I'm taking someone's antique marble collection or something."

"Those can be very valuable, I'll have you know."

"And you know this because, what, someone actually asked you to get his marbles back?"

"Actually, they were his great-grandfather's marbles, which his grandmother had given away after writing her son out of her will."

"And his great-grandson wanted you to track them down all those years later because…"

"Because great-granddad had written about them in his journal, and about the tournaments he'd won with them, both as a kid and a young adult, and he grew really fascinated by them. The shooter that was described in the journal—that's the big marble you use to hit out the other marbles, not a hired gun—was quite famous, amongst those in the sport."

"Which is a relief to know. About the shooter. I mean, I wouldn't think marbles tournaments could be so dangerous, but then I thought I was just retrieving a cell phone this morning."

"Poke fun, but it went on to be a very highly appraised collection, which is currently on display at a museum in Germany."

"So, you actually found it."

He nodded. "One of the more challenging cases I've taken on, but very gratifying and quite fascinating, actually. I didn't know anything about mibology when I took the assignment, but—"

"Mibology?"

"Study of marbles."

She shook her head. "Right. Of course."

"When I took the case, I studied up on that while simultaneously doing the background work on their family tree, and who would have wanted a collection of that caliber. Given that it was well-known, I could only hope someone had bought them up as a set. Then prayed like hell that that person's descendants hadn't gotten rid of them."

"And so you found them and, what, *stole* them from the poor family who'd had them for decades? I mean, they bought them fair and square, right? So—"

He gave her a quelling look. "Of course I didn't steal them. I arranged for the two parties to meet and they came to an equitable solution. More often than not, people are willing to do right by someone else when they know the whole story. Finding things is usually the hardest part."

"See, there you go being all rosily optimistic again."

"Yes, but for every ends-well scenario, you have why the item in question needed to be retrieved in the first place. If Thomas's grandmother hadn't been so punitive in the first place, they'd have passed to him as they should have."

"And you'd be out of a job."

"Exactly. Which is why I said I'm not always the most optimistic person. People can be extraordinarily generous, but they can also be extraordinarily cruel. In my line of work, one is almost always offset by the other."

"At least you give credit where credit is due. And pardon me for assuming you might have 'retrieved' those marbles some other way. Given that I'm presently tied to a chair, I have no idea how I came to that conclusion."

"This…case is different from what I usually do."

"And why are you bending the rules this time?"

"Because there would be no equitable solution between the two parties. Their respective families have been at war with each other for several centuries, with the cruelty far outweighing the kindness. I believed what I'd been told about the rightful ownership of this particular piece of the family's heritage. Instead of going with my gut, I went with what appeared to be the only solid evidence there was regarding its proper placement."

"And you should have trusted your gut."

He nodded.

She was silent for a few moments, then she asked, "What does your gut say about trusting me?"

"I don't know that I have the luxury of relying on instinct in this case."

She leaned back and studied him again, for an even longer moment this time. "You trust me." She smiled. "You can go with your gut on that."

"Sophie—"

She broke in, using possibly the worst New York accent he'd ever heard. "So…when do I make with the break-in, Mugsy?"

Simon slowly dropped his chin to his chest and closed his eyes. "Why is it that doing the right thing is suddenly feeling all kinds of wrong?"

7

"I CAN'T BELIEVE I'm doing this."

"So you've said."

Sophie wriggled around on the other side of Simon's closed
bathroom door, squirming into the maid uniform he'd brought
back, which she purposely hadn't asked how he'd procured.
"If I get the velvet box," she said, her voice muffled by the
not-stretchy-enough black fabric, "then does that mean I can
report to work as usual tonight?"

"It might be best if you lie low until tomorrow. That
would give you time to talk to your friend, find out what
happened."

She stopped midwriggle. "You *want* me to talk to
Delia?"

"Assuming you're not planning on never speaking to her
again, that's going to happen at some point."

"Yeah, but—"

"She's the first one, the main one, who will be suspicious
if she doesn't hear from you."

"I'm sure we're already well past that stage."

"Exactly. So you'll have to contact her, reassure her, follow
up."

"What am I supposed to tell her happened to me?"

"Food poisoning from bad bar food? I don't know."

"There was no food, only alcohol." She struggled to pull the fabric over her hips. "Which is what got me in this situation in the first place," she muttered under her breath. The Wingate family prided themselves on the Old World glamour of their hotels, which precluded their maids from wearing shapeless, one-size-fits-many smocks. They had designed specially made, traditional European-style black maid's outfits, complete with white apron. Their only concession to the comfort of their employees was to allow soft-soled shoes, rather than heels. Sophie had considered it a major coup when the higher-ranking management staff at several of their hotels had pressured the family to include a trouser alternate to the previously mandatory skirt/tailored blazer ensemble for the female management-level employees.

"I'm sure you can come up with something."

"I'm not sure I'm leaving this bathroom, so it might be moot."

"Cold feet?"

"Not cold feet, no. I'm waiting to see if I'll lose a few pounds while arguing with you so that I can get this damn dress down over my butt."

"I thought they were stretchy. They felt stretchy."

She mouthed his words back at him through the closed door, then clamped her teeth down as she gave the fabric a final tug. "They are," she all but growled, which turned into a groan of discomfort as the skirt edged its way past the widest part of her backside, where it finally, mercifully, hung just long enough to brush the back of her thighs.

"Do you need help?"

She refused to look in the mirror. Instead she just opened the door. "Lycra black polyester, two sizes too small. It's what all the fashionable jewel thieves are wearing these days."

She hadn't known what to expect, but the way his gaze immediately raked over her, leaving her feeling almost physically frisked, wasn't it.

"What?" she said, not sure how to take his reaction. His eyes were dark, hot even, and pinned only on her…but he was scowling.

"You're not wearing that."

"I'm pretty sure it will have to be surgically removed, but I'm willing to go under the knife if it means I can breathe again soon." She looked down at herself and grimaced at the way the seams were stretched so far they looked ready to burst. She probably looked like sausage stuffed into casing a link size too small. "If you could get the zipper in the back, I could probably get it from there." A total lie, but maybe he'd leave to find a larger size as she contorted herself into bodily positions no woman should ever be witnessed doing while trying to get the damn thing off.

"Zipper?"

She turned around and shifted her hair to one side.

She thought she heard some kind of strangled noise coming from his throat and tried not to feel insulted. Or hurt. "I pulled the zipper up before tugging the skirt the rest of the way down and I'm fairly certain my arms won't bend that way now without something tearing, popping or becoming dislocated. And I'm not talking about the uniform."

She braced herself for his touch on the back of her neck, but moments passed, and nothing. When he didn't say anything, either, she finally looked over her shoulder at him, which made her gasp slightly as the waist cinched in even further, then gasp again when she spied the expression on his face. "You picked it out, not me," she managed, then turned her back to him again before she turned blue from lack of oxygen. "Zipper. Help. Please."

A moment later his fingertips brushed the sensitive spot on her nape, and she felt like she was being branded. "I think I'm going to lose the use of a lung if you don't get that thing pulled down." In truth, she was more worried about the other reactions her body was having to his touch, and silently willed him to get on with it already.

"I thought uniforms were supposed to be less size specific and more…uniform. I just grabbed one." He held the top of the zipper and carefully began tugging the tag down with his other hand. "Why didn't you just tell me it was too small?"

She didn't say anything. She was too busy holding her breath, and it had nothing to do with the compression on her lungs. He was too close, and his breath was just the right amount of warm on her neck. It made a girl think about things she shouldn't be thinking about just prior to committing her first crime. Okay, okay, technically her second crime, but she honestly didn't feel like a criminal. Until now. They were standing way too close, and plots were being hatched, her heart was pounding, and nefarious deeds were imminent. Wasn't it perfectly normal, then, under that kind of stress, to be thinking about what would happen if he didn't stop with her zipper?

If maybe he leaned in a little closer and pressed those lips to the base of her neck? She gave an involuntary little shiver, and he immediately stopped his seductively slow movement. Yes, it was possible—probable even—that he was just being cautious because of the snug fit, but that didn't fit as well with the scenario playing out in vivid Technicolor in her mind.

"What's wrong?" he asked.

"Nothing," she managed in a choked whisper.

"Is it really that tight?"

She might have whimpered a bit at that, her thoughts not remotely on the fit of the uniform. "Just—pull it the rest of way. Please." She felt the zipper ease down, but her breath didn't return as swiftly. Weren't his fingers lingering a bit too long? Was she imagining that he was still standing too close?

Then his touch was gone. And she sighed a little that the

moment was over. Then his hands came to rest on her waist, his palms spanning it in a way that made her feel petite.

"Sophie."

Just that one word, said in that halting, deeper-than-usual tone, was enough to send a full-body shudder of pure pleasure through her. She pressed her thighs together against the sudden ache there and couldn't have spoken if her life depended on it. She could, however, have stepped away. But she didn't.

"I know I shouldn't be involving you," he said, at length. "Even in a desperate situation, I wouldn't normally compromise—"

"Is it?" she asked, her voice barely more than a hushed whisper. His hands were on her, so it was a miracle she'd found any voice at all. "Desperate, I mean?"

"I'd have found a way to accomplish my goal. I wouldn't be here otherwise."

"But…?"

There was a pause, then she felt rather than heard his intake of breath, as his hands tightened briefly on her waist. "But, nothing. Nothing really excuses putting you in this situation. I'm…" He paused again, then she felt him press his forehead against her hair. She wanted to melt back against him. Nothing in the world would have felt more natural in that moment. "I'm going to let you go," he said.

It wasn't exactly what she wanted to hear, which was when she knew just how much trouble she was really in.

"I'll only ask that you don't tell anyone we met. Fair trade for the early morning intrusion?"

"Simon—"

"I'm here trying to right a wrong. I can't do that by committing another wrong. I should have never let it go this far. You were right, it's not fair. And nothing is so important that I should jeopardize anyone but myself. My timetable for this is quite short, and I—I got carried away, with wanting to fix this before I lose my only shot at it."

She turned then, and his hands stayed on her waist, which meant she was all but in his arms. When she looked up into his eyes, it brought her mouth dangerously close to his. "What if I want to help?"

His eyes searched hers. "You have a smart mouth, Sophie Maplethorpe, but you also have a soft heart. I admire and respect both. But I won't exploit them further."

She was trembling, but not in fear of what she was about to offer. "This morning I was trying to erase a wrong, or, at the very least hide one. I certainly wasn't righting one. But the urgency to fix things—it made me make decisions I otherwise wouldn't have. So I understand more than you know. Earlier, I just wanted to get out of here, with as little fallout as possible. But now—"

"Now nothing has changed."

"Except it has. I know more. About you, about why you're here. I don't know what the whole story is between these two families, but—"

"You don't need to know. That would only put you in more potential danger than you're already in—"

"Potential," she said, and he narrowed his eyes in exasperation, which perversely made her smile. "That means it's not a certainty. What is this person likely to do once you retrieve this velvet box? Will he come after it? After you?"

"Possibly."

"What if he doesn't know it was you?"

"It could only be me. I'm the only one who knows of its real significance, outside of the person I took it from originally."

"Wouldn't he think that person might be after it, then?"

"The original owner is eighty-three and not in the best of health. I doubt it. He knows I know now that I was duped in this. If it disappears, he'll know it's me."

"So, does that mean you look over your shoulder forever?"

"It means I have to get it back to London, to where it

belongs. He won't be able to reach it then. Ever. As for reaching me, he might still think to come after me, to make a point, but he'll know it's a fruitless pursuit otherwise. Once it's done, it's done. Another generation will have to fight over it once they're gone."

"Why is he here with it?"

"To make a vulgar, very well-publicized point of ownership."

"Why not in Britain?"

"He had to know I'd figure things out, so his gloating window is narrow. He won't risk it being seen in public again. But he had to rub Guinn's nose in it, and as he was already planning to attend the international event here, he chose this as his showcase. He even loaned the museum highly-sought after pieces from his rather extensive personal art collection to ensure his high profile while he's here."

She sighed then, trying to think, to sort through things, which was almost impossible given where she was standing at the moment. Then he had to go and scramble what little rational thought she still had left by tipping up her chin with his hand, which he left cupping her face.

"Sophie, stop."

She looked into his eyes. So dark, so serious. "Contrary to what little you know of me, I'm rarely impulsive. I'm not as soft as you think. I do care about my friends. I do care about righting wrongs."

"This isn't your wrong to right."

"Simon—"

He shifted his thumb across her lips, effectively silencing anything else she might have said. "I shouldn't have gotten you involved." He brushed his thumb across her lips.

"Why the sudden shift? You've got me wanting to be on your side now."

"Seeing you in that uniform."

She frowned. "What? Why?"

"Imagining Tolliver seeing you in that uniform." He shook his head. "I'm not putting you anywhere near him."

"In a maid's uniform? No one looks at the maids, trust me."

"A man would have to be dead not to notice you. And that uniform, your curves, the way—" He broke off and shook his head again. "Not happening."

For once, Sophie was speechless. She thought back to the ravenous way he'd raked his gaze over her when she'd come out of the bathroom. And that delicious shiver stole over her once again. He was offering her an out, a chance to walk away. But she was looking at him and he was looking at her, touching her, invading far more than her personal space, and she simply wasn't ready to walk away. Not yet. And in that instant, how Delia could risk everything for a brief thrill came into complete and utter clarity. Heaven help her. "Who is Tolliver?"

His eyes widened for a moment in surprise, then squeezed shut. "See? This is why I work alone. You're a distraction, Sophie, and right now I can't handle a distraction."

"Oh, I'd say we're both already distracted, so we might as well figure out how to make it work for us."

His eyes shot open and she swore she felt the intensity of his gaze all the way down to her toes. "Dangerous talk."

She smiled then. "Danger is my middle name," she said, adopting his accent.

He rolled his eyes, then let out a short, exasperated breath as he shook his head slowly, several times...but he didn't let her go.

"I'm already involved, Simon. I know things. Too many things."

He lifted his head, his expression wary now, and none too happy. "Meaning?"

She lifted one shoulder and aimed for a casual insouciance

she was far from feeling. "Just that, you know, we both still do have something on each other and—"

"I'm not going to jeopardize your job. That's off the table."

"How do I know that?"

He cocked his head. "Are you being serious?"

She really didn't think he'd let her go just to rat her out, she was just trying to find a way to keep him from shoving her out the door. "I'm just saying that we are already in this together, and this is just wasting time. We made a deal, I'm willing to keep my end of the bargain. Your reasons are yours, mine are mine."

"Sophie—"

"Simon," she mimicked. She was fully aware that she was more than a little spellbound by him, fully cognizant that the smart thing to do was to walk out the door and never look back, knew that even if she stayed, it wasn't like he was going to stick around in any capacity. Talk about low percentage outcomes. All risk, no payoff. And there wasn't even any tequila body shots involved to take the brunt of the blame for her continued stupidity.

"Well, then," he said, sighing once again, "I suppose there is only one thing to do."

She sighed as well, partly in relief, and partly to calm her suddenly racing pulse. She was excited. She was terrified. She wasn't leaving. "Which is?"

"Tie you up and keep you here until I see this thing through."

Her mouth dropped open, then snapped shut. *"What?"*

"You heard me. You're too big a risk for me, and I'm not endangering you, either. I'll save you from that fate, even if you won't save yourself."

"I can take care of myself, thank you."

He just cocked his head and gave her a quelling look.

"A bit of pot and kettle, don't you think?" she said, scrambling to figure out what to do next.

"You can call it whatever you want. I momentarily lost my head, but I caught myself in time. I don't know what your reasoning is, but I know I won't use you—"

"Not even my passkey?"

He paused an infinitesimal blink too long.

"It would make the difference, right?" She pulled away from him enough to tug the strap out from where it was trapped inside the uniform. She dragged it over her head. "Here. Use it, then destroy it. I'll file a report saying it was stolen. Covers me from unlawful entry if they tie it to the break-in. If security looks at who was in this room, or gets any suspicions where you're concerned, it won't matter because you'll be long gone by then. Right?"

He just stared at her.

"Will it help you or not? You don't want me in the mix, fine. But let me at least help you get whatever it was you came here for."

"Why?" he asked quietly, his gaze never wavering.

She couldn't tell him the truth. Couldn't tell him that he'd gotten to her, that she was all but a quivering mass of needs and wants at this point and wouldn't have walked away even if she could have recovered whatever part of her brain she'd obviously lost from the moment he'd rolled over in bed, half-naked, and spoken to her. It was wrong, it was stupid, it was the epitome of foolishness, but he was this close to kissing her and, dammit, she wanted—no, needed—to know what it was like to be kissed by Simon Lassiter. Which was a stepping stone away from knowing what it was like to be taken by Simon Lassiter. Shallow? Maybe. Stupid? Surely.

And yet, there she stood, wanting, willing him to lower his mouth, dammit, and just get it over with.

Maybe then she'd get her rationality back and walk away. Maybe.

"I don't know," she lied. Better to lie than make herself any more the fool than she already was.

"What if I'm the bad guy in this? What if you're putting your loyalty in the wrong hands?"

"Like you did, you mean? You said that was because you didn't follow your gut. I am following mine." And the moment she said it, she knew she spoke the absolute truth. Whether her gut was purely hormone-fueled remained to be seen. She couldn't sort that part out at the moment, because he'd shifted his hands from where they palmed her waist again, sliding them down to her hips and sinking his fingertips into the softness there.

She looked up into his eyes. "Are you the bad guy?"

His fingers dug deeper, he pulled her a fraction closer. "Only with you."

"And if I'm agreeing to help, of my own free will? Does that still make you the bad guy?"

"Sophie—"

Before he could say another word, she screwed up the rest of her courage, moved in closer still and blurted, "Now, are you ever going to kiss me?"

His fingers dug in even deeper and he pulled her reflexively closer until their bodies met. And she knew, without any lingering doubts, that those smoldering looks were quite real. *Well, well. Will miracles never cease.*

"No," he said, at length, jaw tight. Rigid even. And it wasn't the only part of him that was rigid…

She just smiled up at him.

He swore. Then crushed his mouth to hers.

8

SHE TASTED SO DAMN GOOD. Better than he'd imagined. And he realized now just how much he'd been imagining this moment. Wanting this moment. She took him, closed her mouth over his, and he was instantly lost in her. She slid her hands through his arms, around his waist, up his back, bringing her gloriously soft body fully against his far harder one as he plundered the depths of her sweet, sweet mouth. He groaned, his hips moving into hers, instinctively seeking what he needed, wanted. Demanded. She moaned, and moved back.

The lust that punched through him was as powerful as it was leveling. The primal need to take, conquer, possess, was something he'd never once felt in his life. Not like this, never like this. The urge so basic, so elemental. So overwhelming. It was a little insane. Hell, his whole life was insane. Nothing made sense any longer. So much was at stake. And all he could think about was sinking more of him into all of her.

From the moment he'd woken up to find her in his room, she'd been a distraction. She wasn't like any woman he'd ever met. Frustrating, compelling, intoxicating. He wanted her. Like he wanted his next breath. He never let himself want anything. Not like this. She'd asked if the situation was desperate. It sure as bloody hell felt that way right that very second.

He should be thinking about the Shay, and only that, but all he could think about was having her, taking her. *Desperate* didn't begin to cover it.

He ripped his mouth from hers, breathing heavily. She bit his chin, slid her hands higher up his back and he wrapped his hand into her hair and pressed her cheek against his shoulder, holding her tight, preventing her from doing anything else until he got some sense of his equilibrium back. Some sense of any kind back. What in the hell was he doing?

"Sophie, this isn't helping matters any. We can't—I can't—"

"Why?" she asked, her voice muffled against his neck, the warmth of her breath alone making his body throb and jump.

Why, indeed.

"It wouldn't serve either of us any purpose," he said, which was perfectly true. And didn't diminish his desire in the slightest.

She tipped her face up to his. "Does everything have to have a purpose?"

His body was right on board with that line of reasoning. He struggled to rise above those baser demands. "No, but this seems particularly counterproductive."

"To your mission, you mean?"

"To…anything. Yes, to my reason for being here, but yes to every other reason as well." He needed to set her away from him, step back. But then he'd just see her in that ridiculous excuse for a uniform and fling her on the nearest bed. "I'm here for a short time, you're permanent, and nothing is going to change that. I'm not one to pursue things just because they're in front of me."

"I'm not, either," she said, sounding quite sincere.

"Well, then?"

"I haven't been behaving normally all day. Why start now?" She smiled then. "I'm certainly undermining any position I might have had to give Delia a lecture on the consequences of impulsive behavior, but I'll deal with that when the time comes."

He framed her face, felt her soft hair curl around his finger. His body responded by growing that much harder and he felt his throat go dry from the need to taste her again. He was like a starving man, and there was only one thing that would sate his appetite. "Does this have something to do with that? With losing your friend to marriage?" *Keep talking,* he schooled himself. *Until you can let her go.*

"I'm not losing my friend to marriage, I'm losing her to the Wingate family, and that process started some time ago. I'm not any happier about it now, but it certainly isn't provoking me to aberrant behavior."

Aberrant behavior. That was certainly one way to sum up this entire morning. "Do you envy her her fling last night, then?"

"No, of course not."

But he noticed she had looked away then.

He shifted her face back to his and looked into her eyes. "Never play poker," he advised.

"Maybe I do envy her a little," she admitted. "Not the cheating part. I would never do that. But the abandon, maybe. The throwing caution to the wind and just doing what felt right. Without the tequila, of course. I wouldn't want any regrets."

"No, of course not."

She looked directly into his eyes then and his own dry smile was reflected in her own. "I'm well aware this falls squarely under the heading of being careful what you wish for." She reached up and covered his hand with her own, pressing his palm more tightly against her cheek. "But that doesn't keep me from wishing, all the same."

"Why" he asked, quite seriously. "Simply for the thrill?"

She slid her hand from his and touched her fingers to his face. He felt his heart tighten, literally, inside his chest.

"I'm not a thrill seeker, Simon. I'm...I'm the good girl. The one who does the right thing. Helps her friends, focuses on her career. Makes the smart decisions. But just this once..." She trailed off, sighed.

"Just this once...what?" he prodded, knowing he should let it go, but unable to do the smart thing, either.

"I want to go after what I want, even if the only reason is because I just want to. No smart deliberations, no careful analysis, just pure, unadulterated immediate gratification."

Now more than his heart tightened. "And then what?"

"I don't know. I guess...I want that not to matter either, for once. Can't I just reach out and take what's in front of me, and damn the consequences?"

She traced her fingers down his cheek, along his jaw, and he felt the trembling. She was trembling.

"Can't you, Simon?"

He turned his head so that her hand brushed across his lips, pulled a fingertip between his lips...and sucked on it. It was a short, dark slide into the whirlpool, and he was rapidly losing whatever control he had that would prevent him from taking that primal dive. Headfirst.

She gasped, and he let her finger slide from his mouth...and replaced it with her lips. She immediately opened to him, and he slid his tongue into her mouth, tasting, reveling...sinking deeper, faster.

Her arms went around his neck, her fingers slid up into his hair, her nails raking his scalp as she urged his mouth closer, tighter, took his tongue deeper.

He groaned from somewhere deep inside his chest...and let her. Pulling her tightly into his arms, he shifted them both until her back was against the wall next to the bathroom door. If it wasn't for the damn dress, he'd have slid her higher, wrapped her legs around his waist. As it was, he settled for sinking his hips into her perfectly soft ones. She groaned this time, and he was right on the verge of spinning them both around and finding the bed…or the floor, when sanity finally prevailed. He had one chance to fix what he'd done…. What the hell did he think he was doing?

He slid his mouth from hers, then tucked her close against his shoulder, burying his face in her hair while he tried to regain what was left of his perspective. "Sophie, I shouldn't have, we—"

"It's okay," she said, her voice husky and sexy as hell. "I know. I…I know."

He could feel her heart pound against his chest and felt his own twist a little. Why couldn't things be uncomplicated? Consenting adults who just wanted to go for the moment. But he'd already made one mistake that had sent him here in the first place. The last thing he was going to do was compound that by making another. And while taking Sophie Maplethorpe might be about the finest way to spend an afternoon that he could think of, there was no question it would be a mistake. And it wasn't just her best interests he was looking out for. He was in way over his head here…and he'd never so much as had to tread water before in his life. Best to wade right back out, right now.

"If it's of any comfort," he said, at length, "I'd prefer not to let you go. I'd much rather my agenda for the day have nothing to do with Tolliver and that velvet case, and everything to do with granting you your wish for flinging with abandon."

He felt rather than heard her responding sigh. "That does sound like a much better way to spend the day." Her tone was resigned.

He brushed her curls back from her forehead, wishing he could stem the wave of regret. "And then the day would end, and I would need to head home."

"Mmm," she said.

"Mmm, indeed." He framed her face with his hands, her curls dancing over his fingers. "And I'm afraid I wouldn't like that part at all."

"No," she said, her voice low, more subdued than he'd ever heard it. "Not at all."

"So, we're in agreement, then. No flinging, with or without abandon."

She sighed a little, and pressed her cheek into his palm. "I suppose not."

"I'm not happy about it," he added, not making the slightest effort to release her.

"Me, either."

And then she lifted her gaze to his, those soft gray eyes so transparent with want and need—of him. Her lips parted, and waiting.

And his mouth was on hers again before he could question the action, much less the dangerous line he was crossing. Leaping past, in fact.

Her hands were instantly clutching fistfuls of his shirt, and she clung to him as he took the kiss deeper. He moaned, or she did, perhaps they both did. He quickly lost any sense of place, or time. It was only when he tried to pull her thighs up to brace against his that they were both caught up short by the limitations of her dress.

She was already unbuttoning his shirt, but they were both forced to pause when the skirt of her uniform refused to slide so much as an inch upward.

"Cut it off," she demanded while tugging his shirt from his waistband.

The adamant demand made him chuckle.

"If you were in the male equivalent of this get-up right now, trust me, you wouldn't be laughing."

"Oh, I agree. And I've never wished more that I was the swashbuckling hero with a knife strapped to his hip, so I could grant your demand."

"You have a gun strapped to your ankle," she said, panting. "So it wasn't an entirely unreasonable request."

"I thought you weren't a thrill seeker."

"I could name a dozen reasons just off the top of my head that would make any woman want to have you slice the clothes right off her that have nothing to do with your job description." She flipped open another button. "Although if there is an adrenaline rush anything close to this that comes with the job you do, then go ahead and sign me up full-time."

"Generally, it's not all that exciting." He pressed his body closer to hers, effectively stopping her attempts to undress him. He waited until she lifted her gaze to his. "I must admit, though, there's never been a rush quite like you."

She went soft then. "Oh, Simon."

"I have a job to do here, Sophie. And all I can think about is what I'd like to do to you."

His words made her lips part and his gaze dipped to her mouth, wanting nothing so much as to sink himself into it again. And again. And then far beyond her mouth.

"Maybe that's all the purpose we need," she said.

"You're not helping me regain control of the situation here."

She smiled a little then, and his heart tipped further. "And you're not helping me get you out of this shirt. We all have our burdens to bear."

"For someone who doesn't typically fling, you've taken to the lifestyle quite famously, I'll have you know."

"Well, I'm rather indecently inspired."

He groaned and tipped his head to hers. "First I turn you to a life of crime, now I'm inspiring indecency."

"I turned myself to crime, if you recall, and as for the indecency, well, that will only be a crime if you don't follow through with what you started."

"Sophie—"

"Simon."

When he simply shook his head, she finally used her nose to nudge up his chin so he was looking at her again. "Do you really think we're not going to end up naked at some point?"

"I don't know what to think, except—"

"How about I go retrieve that velvet box. Then, when I come back, we can discuss things further. Once you have what you've come here for, then anything else we decide is just about what we want. Right?"

He looked into sparkling eyes set into such a perfectly innocent-looking face, processing the very un-innocent proposal she was making…and finding it almost impossible to say no. In fact, it sounded like the most splendid proposal ever. Until he allowed himself to get to the part where he'd have to leave her to head back to England. Leaving her now, half-dressed in this maid uniform was already proving to be next to impossible. How much harder would it be to leave the soft warmth of all of her?

"We'll have regrets," he said.

"Almost definitely."

"Then why do it?"

"Because I'll regret more not following through. I don't feel like this often. Okay, ever. And I realize we may be all wrapped up in the external drama of our chance encounter, and maybe that's the fuel behind all of this. But that's how it happened. And here we are. And now…now I want what I want. I'd have regrets either way."

"Even if having more just makes you want more?"

"See, you say things like that to me and how am I supposed to walk away without even trying to find out what might be?"

"Nothing can be. We're relative strangers, caught up in an otherwise inexplicable situation, who happen to discover there is a little chemistry—"

"A little chemistry," she echoed, trailing soft fingertips over his skin.

"Sophie."

"Simon."

He sighed. Again. "The thing is, I've never met anyone like you. You say the damnedest things, and you somehow manage to engage all of my attention, and you look like this Venetian goddess or something—"

Now she sighed, and it was quite languorous and heartfelt. "Seriously, you keep up with that and I'm packing myself in your suitcase and going back to England with you."

And that's when he knew just how serious, how dangerous, she'd truly become to him. Because, even teasingly, the very idea of it had his pulse leaping, and this kernel of hope blooming. He was not the pulse-leaping, hope-blooming type. He was steady, and forward moving, and all about getting the job done and done well. Somewhere in there he supposed he'd hoped he'd stumble across someone who would turn both his head and his heart, and then be willing to put up with him and his unusual lifestyle...but he'd never expected to stumble quite like this.

And he'd never expected anything like her.

"Whatever am I to do about you?" he asked, unsure if he was asking her...or himself.

"You're to go and find me a proper-fitting maid uniform, then we're going to retrieve that box. Then, if I have my way, we're going to fling. With absolute abandon." She toyed with the remaining closed buttons to his shirt.

"What have I gone and done?"

"You'll have gone and done me, I hope," she said, flushing furiously even as she grinned. "Right after we get that box back."

9

SOPHIE KEPT HER SUPPLY CART directly in front of her and her face averted from any potential passersby. Her uniform was at least two sizes too big now. She had her hair pinned up and under a net, as well as a pair of black-framed reading glasses Simon had picked up in one of the hotel's boutiques. Not the greatest disguise in the world, but the day shift people didn't know her all that well, and certainly wouldn't notice her dressed like this. And she'd been in the business long enough to know that guests didn't really pay any attention to the maid service personnel.

Still, she felt naked, exposed, and very much like there was a neon sign flashing over her head saying, "Thief! Idiot! Stop her!"

The thing was, she was out of the room now. Free to run, to report Simon to security, to hide until this all blew over, or any number of other options. And here she was, with the cart and her passkey, repeating Tolliver's room number, over and over, in her head. Probably not the option most would recommend.

Sure, she could blame it on a hormonal fog, and she didn't think a jury of her peers—especially the female members—

would convict her if they got a look at her partner in crime. Still.

"Shallow. Superficial. Stupid," she muttered. Except she wasn't generally any of those things. She was the steady one. The levelheaded one. That was why she and Delia had hit it off so well. Delia was the fun-loving sprite to Sophie's levelheaded calm. They were both smart women, with very specific goals, but the way they tackled them was diametrically opposite…and that's what they enjoyed about each other. That vicarious thrill of being around the person they might wish they were. At least some of the time.

Even someone who looked and sounded like Simon wouldn't normally cause her to act like she didn't have a brain in her head. Okay, so a man who looked and sounded like Simon had never once strolled into her life. But she was fairly certain, on a normal day, she might have gazed longingly, fantasized a little, and then gotten back to work.

There was more to this than the fact that a guy like him had actually noticed a woman like her. That was only part of why she was preparing to commit her second crime in twenty-four hours. There was more to it with him, more *to* him. As he'd spoken of his parents' relationship, and, later, of his occupation, there had been something sincere and earnest in the way he talked of those things. She understood he felt somewhat jaded by the exposure his job afforded him to the less than generous spirits of some people, but maybe he was too close to it to realize just how clearly hopeful he remained. It was obvious in the very reason he was here, risking everything to right a wrong. And she could help him make that happen.

She pushed the cart doggedly down the hall, creeping ever closer to Suite 1671. Her mind went back to when Simon had pushed her up against the wall, when he was taking her with kisses so intense, so focused, so…damn good. What might have happened had she been wearing anything other than that tourniquet of a uniform?

Afterward, when they'd finally taken their hands off each other, they'd discussed her involvement. Okay, so they'd heatedly argued about her involvement. He'd made his case with a list of all the reasons why she should walk away and never look back. She'd fired back by throwing his own initial explanation of why he'd needed her help in his face.

And…here she was, with the cart. And the key. So, she supposed she'd won. Although, at the moment, every one of Simon's reasons were perversely echoing through her mind. She didn't want to know what was going through his mind. She'd left him pacing his hotel room like a caged panther. She thought about going back to that pacing panther, velvet box in hand. Ready for reward time.

She rolled her cart to a stop, knowing she should be vowing to never again let her work life consume her personal life to the point where grand larceny and a nooner seemed like a wise thing to do. Except, what were the chances that combination would ever present itself to her again?

And what were the chances she'd ever again meet anyone like Simon Lassiter?

She paused a few feet from the door and took several measured breaths to steady her nerves. Even if Simon hadn't been ridiculously sexy, she'd like to believe she'd have still helped him out. A beacon of altruism, that was her.

Before that beacon flickered out, she slipped her passkey over her head and slid it through the door lock. It flickered green and the lock retracted. Heart pounding, stomach churning, she took a deep breath, pushed her glasses up the bridge of her nose and pasted what she hoped was a nondescript, pleasant smile on her face. "Housekeeping," she called out, not overly loudly, hoping, praying, that she wasn't going to interrupt anything she shouldn't be interrupting.

She was breaking strict hotel protocol by entering a room without ascertaining either a lack of occupancy, or the verbal agreement of the residing hotel guest, but then, she wasn't hoping for vacancy and she wasn't about to give the resident guest a chance to turn down maid service. At least not until she got a good look at the room. She could always claim she'd called out and didn't hear the response.

Simon had told her where to look first, even if all she got to do was a quick, visual scan. She was supposed to try and talk her way into the room if stopped too soon once inside the door, claim she needed to put in fresh towels, anything that would allow her to scope out as much of the suite as possible.

Of course, with her milkmaid skin, it was next to impossible to pretend any kind of language barrier as a means of misunderstanding his potential refusal of her services. Simon had suggested maybe a Russian accent, or something Nordic, but that had lasted all of two attempts, both ending with her dissolving in laughter after sounding like Natasha from an old Bullwinkle cartoon. She'd just have to brazen it out, while trying to be as inconspicuous and unremarkable as possible.

The door swung inward and she flipped the doorstop down to keep it propped open. Her cart was clearly visible from inside the room, but not entirely blocking the door. Her only escape route.

"Housekeeping," she said again, hefting a stack of bath towels into her arms before stepping farther into the room. There were the remains of a room service breakfast on the table in the main room, a newspaper refolded on the adjoining chair. Service for two, she noted, her gaze darting back and forth, waiting for imminent discovery. It was only when her heart stopped threatening to pound straight through her eardrums that she heard the shower running through the open door to the bedroom. Wow. Bonus. This might be easier than she'd thought it would be. She grinned as she made her way farther into the front room, then froze when she heard the noises— male grunting and female giggling—from the other side of the bathroom door. Which was across the room, through the bedroom, on the opposite wall. Over running water. Clearly.

So, Tolliver and his "associate" were showering together. Of the full-contact variety. It was just as well she didn't know what either of them looked like. That was a visual she could do without pondering while trying to master her new stealth skills. Which left her imagination wide open to picture an entirely different version of the scenario, complete with Simon and the walk-in shower she knew these rooms sported, which she quickly moved to quash. She had no idea how long they'd been in there, but things sounded like they were...culminating. At least she'd have a few seconds' warning when the shower kicked off. Because she highly doubted when they opened the door, either one of them would be pleased to find a maid standing there. Even if she did have some nice, dry towels waiting for them.

Yeah. Better get to work. A quick scan of both dressers, inside and out, and the dressing area—boy, Tolliver's significant giggler must have stock in MAC cosmetics—didn't reveal any velvet cases. In fact, despite the counter full of makeup and closet stuffed with more shoes and clothes than Sophie owned, much less traveled with, there was something noticeable missing from the tableau. Jewelry. Not even a man's wristwatch on the nightstand or dresser top.

She went to the closet where the room safe was, and carefully crouched down, still clutching the towels, to do a quick rattle of the handle and check of the dial. It was in use. "Dammit."

The guest set his own numbers with each use, which meant she had no access to that information, and security had the only override codes, for use when the guest forgot what numbers they'd chosen.

The decibel level in the bathroom really started to climb, and, trying not to cringe—they were just on the other side of the closet wall, ew—she started to straighten, but the towels squished down when she pressed on them for leverage, throwing her balance off, sending her sprawling back into a sea of strappy, bejeweled Paciottis and red-soled Louboutins. Sophie swore, but briefly wondered if she and the water-nymph were the same shoe size.

And then the shower cut off.

Crap!

The closet was across the room from the door leading to the main living area. About as far from safety as she could be. She scrambled to her knees, swearing under her breath as the heels stabbed into her flesh, and finally got into a crouch position, towels dangerously close to erupting from her arms. *Think, think!* Did she try and sprint to the door and hope they were too…involved to notice as she ducked out of the bedroom? It was that, or hide in the closet, which was likely their next destination. She glanced out the closet door across the wide expanse of unmade bed and made a face. She hoped, anyway. Which left sprinting or brazening it out. She couldn't come up with a good reason why she was in their closet with an armful of towels, so that didn't seem wise. So, sprint it was.

Even without the towels, she'd have been handicapped. She'd never been good at sports in school. Any sports, but especially those that involved running. Her body was not designed for quick, efficient movement. Her body….bounced. A lot. But even Ms. Hadrington, her seventh-grade gym teacher, whom Sophie privately thought would have had a much better career with the WWF, would have been proud of her right then, when Medford Middle School's worst athlete ever did the ten-yard dash in under five seconds, all without losing a single towel.

Sophie teetered into the main room and was just rounding the coffee table, her cart in sight through the open hallway door, when a man's voice, crisply British, stopped her cold.

"Who's out there?" And he sounded really threatening. "Who is in my room!"

Iced terror filled her veins where moments ago, nice, warm life-giving blood had been flowing. What in the hell had she been thinking that she could pull something like this off? Why hadn't she listened to Simon and his stupid list?

"Housekeeping," she squeaked, far more out of breath than her short dash excused.

"Stop right there," came a voice from behind her. Tolliver. Still not happy.

She froze, clutching the towels, keeping her face averted as she cleared her throat. "So sorry, I intrude," she said, the Russian accent just popping out of nowhere. Flight or fight instinct, she guessed. And now she had to go with it. "I bring towels. Change your linens?" She still had her back half turned to him and kept the stack of towels up in front of her, mostly hiding her face.

"Does the Wingate Hotel make a habit of allowing its cleaning staff into rooms while occupied?"

"I—announce myself. Hear nothing." She sounded like Natasha on helium, her voice was so squeaky high. Abject terror did that to a person apparently. When he said nothing, she added, "I come in, hear shower, erm, laughter, and leave quick." She ducked her head, not having to fake the furious blush.

"I don't appreciate the uninvited intrusion," he barked. "In fact, I have half a mind to call your superior."

"No, no, please don't. First day," she said, keeping her chin bowed. "I sorry. Will no happen again." Her accent had taken on some kind of weird Asian flair now. She had to get out of there.

"Don't they train you people?"

You people? She almost raised her head and turned toward him, prepared to defend her hotel and its very well-trained staff. Thankfully, his continued rant gave her a chance to check the instinctive action.

"I expected better of a five-star hotel. I thought the Wingate prided itself on its atmosphere. Well, I can tell you, I certainly don't like the atmosphere right at the moment, my door wide open, and someone in my room while I'm showering."

"Very sorry," she said, gritting her teeth.

"In the future, kindly wait until the room is empty before stepping foot in here, or I'll see to it you're looking for a new career."

The viselike grip of terror on her heart started to ease up. She was going to get out of here. She nodded with vigor and started to take mincing, subservient steps closer to the hallway door.

"Leave the towels on the table there."

"Yes, sir," she said, trying to angle herself in such a way to prevent him from having clear view of her face, now that she'd lost her shield. "Again, so sorry."

"Idiot labor," he muttered. "Same all over the world."

Her steps stuttered slightly, only a few feet from freedom. And it was suddenly all she could do to keep from snatching the "Do Not Disturb" sign off the inside door handle and winging it at him. *Just get out in the hall, and out of this room.* But she couldn't seem to help herself. She slipped the sign from the handle.

"Tolly?" A woman's voice floated from the steamy depths of the bathroom. "I need help, baby. Come dry my back." This was followed by another trilling giggle that made Sophie's ears hurt.

She risked a glance back at Tolliver, getting her first real look at him. He was significantly older than she'd thought. And didn't do a damn thing for the hotel towel wrapped around his waist. She thought about the squealer in the other room, and wondered about women who found older men—much older men—attractive. She would guess the attraction had more to do with his net worth than his— She stopped that train of thought right there and looked away from the sunken chest and liver spots. It took all kinds, she supposed, but she wasn't that kind.

Tolliver waved his hand at her dismissively, then disappeared back into the bedroom. No ass to speak of either, she noted. And yet he'd had no problem commanding the room, and her attention, quite easily, despite his less than commanding visual presence. His voice had that kind of soulless chill she'd noted lacking in Simon straight off. She'd prefer not to tangle with Tolliver or his liver spots again, she knew that much.

She put the sign on the outside door handle before closing it behind her, then gripped her cart white-knuckled as she pressed her forehead against a stack of wrapped toilet paper. The adrenaline continued to pump, making her feel a little queasy. "Idiot labor," she muttered. "Jerk. How about idiot arm candy girlfriend? And idiot old man needing an ego boost?" Probably not all he needed boosted, she thought, uncharitably. He was just as pathetic as his squealer girlfriend who was probably less than a third his age.

Just then the door across the hall opened. "Miss?"

Sophie straightened immediately, having to jam the glasses on her nose before they slid off. *"Si?"* Si? What, now she was suddenly Hispanic?

A middle-aged woman in a business suit stood in the doorway, trying to keep it open with her heel while simultaneously putting in her earrings. "Could I trouble you to do a quick cleanup? Bath, bed, the works?" She didn't wait for an answer, but hustled back inside, then reappeared with a briefcase a moment later. "I've got a sales meeting in five, and if all goes well, I won't be returning to my room alone." She shot Sophie a grin. "Thanks!" Then she took off down the hall at a half trot, fluffing her hair and smacking the lipstick on her lips.

"Mas que feliz," Sophie said with a little wave to the rapidly disappearing woman. She could only hope she'd been as invisible to Tolliver. "Lovely. Everyone is getting action but me. Even Tolliver." *Gah*.

Then, realizing she was still standing in the hallway outside his door, she quickly trundled her cart the opposite way from the other guest, toward the service elevator. She used the house phone and her newly honed Russian-Asian-Spanish accent skills, and called in a service request for the room across from Tolliver's, then took the service elevator down two floors, abandoned the cart and ducked into the stairwell to make the rest of the descent to the seventh floor and back to Simon's room.

She was out of breath by the time she got there. He all but yanked the door open and dragged her into the room before she could slide her passkey along the lock. He pushed the door shut and pulled her farther into the room.

"Slow down, cowboy." She untangled her arm from his grip.

"How did it go? What happened? I should have never let you go in there." He raked a hand through his already thoroughly overly raked hair. He really had been worried.

"No velvet box. Nothing happened. And I couldn't agree with you more."

"No box? Nothing? Wait—what?"

"Stupidest thing I've done since, well, earlier today, I guess." She sank down on the side of the bed, her legs suddenly the consistency of sea foam. "I am so not cut out for this. You were right, Simon. And then, Tolliver almost catches me knee-deep in his closet, fiddling with the safe, and out of nowhere I start with the Russian accent—which gets better under duress, I'm happy to report. Not so much with the Asian dialect. Although I'm pretty good with Spanish."

"What?" Simon stopped pacing in front of her. "Wait, Tolliver almost caught you? In his closet? I thought you said nothing happened."

"Nothing did. Almost happened isn't the same thing as actually happened."

Simon sank down next to her on the bed. "Start to finish. Go."

She couldn't help it, she leaned against him. Sure, she'd come back empty-handed, and given his present level of anxiety and the current state of her stomach, not to mention her spongy knees, her streak of not getting lucky probably wasn't about to change. But that didn't mean she couldn't lean. For a moment.

"You didn't tell me he was so old. Or that his roomie was so young."

"They're always young. And what difference does that make?"

"None, just that it was kind of a jolt seeing him in that towel, and looking at that and thinking about the ridiculous giggling and—"

"Why in hell were you with Tolliver in a towel?"

"Calm down." Although a part of her undeniably perked up a little at the implied possessiveness. She hated jealous men. But on Simon it was kind of hot. And a little sweet. "He—Tolliver—was in the towel," she said, leaning again. "I was just carrying them. When I got there, Tolliver and model-of-the-moment were taking a shower. Together. With clear audio."

She felt him shudder a little. "Oh."

"I know." She rubbed her arms. "But I thought it was good luck for me, because then I had free reign in the room without them knowing I was even there. I figured the shower getting turned off would be my signal to scoot, or at least get back to doing something maidly."

"Maidly?"

"Technical term."

His lips twitched, even though she could feel that his body was still singing with tension. "So, what happened?"

"I didn't see the velvet box anywhere, or, for that matter, any jewelry, which led me to think he was using the room safe. Which is in the closet. It was hard to balance with all the towels—"

"What towels? What closet were you in?"

"The walk-in closet. The towels were my cover."

"Your…cover."

"Right. Anyway, I was trying to crouch down and check to see if the safe was in use—don't even ask for the code, the guest can set his or her own—and it looked like it was being used. Then I lost my balance, sprawled all over Miss Universe's vast shoe collection, and that's when the shower went off."

Simon straightened. "What did you do?"

"I managed to get into the other room before he stopped me—"

He turned to her. "Stopped you how?"

"By saying the word 'stop.'" She looked at him. "Are you really so anal, or just big into micromanaging?"

"I work alone," he said. "And I'm never anal."

"So, why the third degree every time I mention Tolliver?"

His shoulders relaxed slightly, but the intensity in his gaze didn't diminish one bit. "I don't like you anywhere around him."

"If you're worried I might become a squealer-in-waiting, don't. Besides, I doubt I'm his type. I can actually think and speak in full sentences."

"I'm not worried about you—not in that way—it's Tolliver."

"I can assure you he's not my type, either."

"That wouldn't necessarily stop him if he thought you had something he could use."

"What, you think he'd jump me or something? He can't know I'm working with you."

Simon swore and abruptly stood, leaving Sophie to catch herself before falling over. "I don't know what in the hell is wrong with me." He paced to the window. "I shouldn't have sent you in there." He turned. "Did he get a clear look at you?"

"No, not really. I had to leave the towels on the table right before I stepped out, and that was the only time we had a clear view of each other. I could have done without that, but I seriously doubt he's the type to pay attention to the 'idiot help' as he called me."

"He notices more than you'd think."

"I think he needed to get back to Suzi or Candi and dry her back. I don't think he paid any attention to me."

Simon said nothing, but continued to pace.

"I'm sorry I couldn't find it. I'm guessing that was why he was so outraged to find hotel staff in his room. Because he had something to hide."

"Possibly. He's not the easiest man under any circumstances." He paced back. "You said you looked in the drawers, everything?"

"Wherever I thought he might stash an invaluable antique. Like I said, there were all the usual trappings of guests. Clothes, shoes, makeup—oh my god, the cosmetics she uses. But not a piece of jewelry. Not so much as a watch on the dresser or nightstand. I thought that was odd."

"Tolliver uses a pocket watch."

Sophie didn't ask how he knew that. She'd been begging for more to the story all along, but he was agitated enough at the moment that she doubted now would be the time.

"Still, with the shoes, the designer clothes, the makeup, I'd have expected his partner would have been decked out with a jewelry store's worth, at the least."

"In the safe, I'm guessing."

"Probably."

Simon finally stopped pacing and came to sit beside her again. He surprised her by turning her face to his, his touch far more gentle than his demeanor or his expression, which was still quite intense. "Thank you for being willing to help.

This…situation is out of your league. I knew that, there was no excuse. I'm sorry I let you go in there. I never should have—"

She silenced him with a kiss.

"Sophie—"

"It's over. At least my part. I'm safe, okay?" She kissed him again, then paused when he continued to hold back. With her lips against his, she whispered, "Simon…please."

And that was all it took.

His mouth was on her, her hands were on him. He plucked her glasses off and tossed them in the general direction of the nightstand. Her hairnet followed. And then he was kissing the side of her neck, his hands spearing through her tangled curls as he lowered her back down on the bed.

She started unbuttoning his shirt.

"Sophie…"

"If you think I'm going to stop, think again," she said, yanking his shirt free of his waistband.

When he stopped kissing her shoulder, and started to lift his head, she dragged his mouth right back down again. "Your conscience isn't going to get the better of you for at least another…thirty minutes."

Then he did lift his head, and the most glorious grin was creasing his handsome face. "Only thirty minutes?"

Wow. She might die from the pleasure of that broad, open grin alone. But at least she was going to be mighty happy in heaven.

"I'll let you decide," she said, and pulled his mouth to hers.

10

HE HAD NO COMMON SENSE left when it came to Sophie. He wasn't the possessive, controlling sort. Far from it. And yet there was no denying she'd roused a little of both in him, without even trying. Okay, maybe more than a little. And despite telling himself that he wasn't going to touch her again, his hands were all over her, as was his mouth. That's where he'd wanted them to be, if he were completely honest, since shortly after he'd blinked his eyes open at the crack of dawn this morning to find her crouching by his bed, her hand shoved into the chair cushion, and a guilty expression all over her incredibly adorable face.

He didn't even know her, not in any real sense, but what he did know was as intriguing as it was intoxicating. She had a smart mouth and oh-so-vulnerable gray eyes. She was confident and clever, and yet a more self-deprecating woman he'd never met. She seemed to think she was invisible, and yet she had the body of siren and the face of an angel. He couldn't find any equilibrium around her, much less exhibit even the least bit of rational thought. She'd left him aroused, disconcerted, anxious and a little pissed off. All of which—the fact that she could even do that to him—bothered him. Pacing the floor while she was gone, being more nervous, scared even, than he could ever recall being, had only amped up those emotions.

And as he slid his hand under her to tug at the zipper, he knew he wasn't going to be rational about this anytime soon. Maybe if he got a taste of her, it would help him to put her—this—in perspective, to get some kind of balance back, get himself back into the mind-set he absolutely had to be in, if he was going to outwit Tolliver and get Guinn his damn emerald. Back to where he'd been right up until the moment he'd caught her breaking into his room.

Her hands were slipping around his waistband as she pulled his shirt the rest of the way free, and his body leaped to full, erect attention. He stopped tangling with her zipper and pulled her hands away, pinning them next to her head. Her cheeks were flushed, her eyes glittering with desire and sheer joy, and he'd never, ever, wanted anything or anyone so badly in his entire life.

He let out a long sigh.

"Don't," she said, wariness creeping into her expression.

"I don't want to stop," he assured her.

"Simple solution. Don't."

"I'm being completely honest when I say that I've never wanted to continue, with such great enthusiasm, and for as long as I could hold out, possibly ever."

"Don't let me interrupt, then."

"Sophie—"

"Simon."

He pressed his forehead to hers. "You are impossibly enticing."

She laughed at that, a purely delighted sound that only served to bring him to an even more urgent state.

"Why, because I say your name in a pleading whine?"

"Because you look like innocence personified, and yet…" He slid his hands down her arms, and along the ample curves of her body. "You feel like the most sinful thing I've ever—"

"Simon," she said, only this time her eyes had drifted shut, and her voice had taken on a distinct needy, breathy quality as she arched into him, urging him to continue his exploration.

"I have work to do," he said, his hands still moving down along the sides of her hips, along her thighs. His body begged for release. "Serious, important work."

"I know. And I'm still willing to help."

"Don't be," he said, leaning in and taking a long, lingering taste of the slender white column of her neck, so beautifully presented to him as she arched further, pushing her head back into the mattress.

He didn't want to think about what he'd done, what he'd gotten her to do. He just wanted more of this…this mindless exploration, this giving in to the basic demands of need and want. He should be worried about what she'd expect afterward, from him, but realized, in that moment, that he was far more concerned with what he'd want. From her.

His mind hung on that, even as he slid his hands up her thighs, pushing her ridiculous uniform up as he went. He moved his body down over hers, trailing nips and kisses along her now exposed shoulder, which was just as damnably soft and sweet as the rest of what he'd discovered thus far.

There could be no relationship, of course. Their lives were far too divergent. She seemed to be okay, taking this for what it was, a crazy chance encounter that they, two consenting adults, were simply taking full advantage of. Why he couldn't get his head in that same place, he had no idea. But he knew, the more carnal knowledge he had of Sophie, the more knowledge he'd crave, of all kinds. Anything to do with her, her wants, needs, hopes, dreams, he'd want to know all about it. Hell, he already did.

She was writhing now, as his hands slipped up over her hips, under the uniform skirt, only to discover something

quite flimsy and lacy. He didn't know why that surprised him.
She was, in every way, intensely female. He supposed it was
her no-nonsense talk, the way she viewed the world and had
no problem expressing those views and expecting others to
concur with her adroit conclusions. She wasn't always careful with her mouth, and he liked that about her. Dear God,
he liked all kinds of things about that mouth. Her tongue, so
sharp at times, so at odds with her innocent Bambi eyes and
pale, soft skin. He wanted her to do all kinds of things with
that tongue.

Then there was the rest of her body, made for a man to sink
himself into, every aching inch. He could only imagine how
bloody fantastic she was going to feel wrapped around him,
holding him deep inside her, and he wanted to find that out
more than he wanted his next breath. Which, given how hard
his heart was pounding, was becoming increasingly difficult,
the more he explored.

He slid farther down as he pushed the skirt up higher still,
until he could see the soft pink cotton, trimmed with lace,
and a tiny bow, right where he wanted to press a deep kiss...
before moving lower. He kissed just below her navel, making
her gasp and pump her hips. He wrapped his hands around her
hips, his fingers sinking into the softness of her lush backside
as he urged her upward, and pulled at the tiny bow with his
teeth.

"Simon," she said, the word more gasp than anything.

"Mmm" was all he could manage, as he breathed in the
scent of her, so ready for him, for everything he wanted to do
to her, with her.

He tugged at the bow with his teeth, pulling it down, using
his hands to slide the tiny straps down over the soft flesh of
her hips and thighs.

She gasped and her hips jolted when he kissed her inti-
mately, then she groaned in deep appreciation as he slid his
tongue over her...and deep into her. Her hips jerked, then

quickly found a rhythm with his strokes, short, heavy gasps alternated with long, appreciative moans, until she was writhing beneath him, slender fingers buried in his hair, holding on for sweet life as he took her, trembling, shaking, over the edge. He pressed kisses along the soft skin of her inner thigh as the quakes continued to roll over and through her, deeply gratified that he'd brought her such pleasure. He looked up, expecting to find her head tipped back, eyes squeezed shut, only to find her looking steadily at him, lips parted, and a somewhat stunned expression on her lovely face.

A warmth filled him then, a kind of pervasive spreading of joy that was quite insidious. Yes, he'd given her an orgasm. First try. Not bad. In fact, he was damn happy, and hopeful for a repeat performance. But that wasn't what the joy was all about. More an aftereffect, proof of what he'd already suspected. Which was that partnering Sophie—in anything—was likely to always be an enlightening and particularly satisfying endeavor.

Then she let him go and reached for his shoulders, sinking her fingers in and trying to pull him up. "Come here," she said, her voice all husky and sweet. "You give great prelude, you know, but there's more. The more you might be particularly interested in."

"Sophie, wait—"

"I couldn't be a safer partner," she assured him. "I'd show you my medical records, but that might kill the mood a bit, given I don't carry them on me. I know you have no reason to just believe—"

"That's not it."

She tipped up her head and looked at him. "Then what is it? If it's protection, well, I'm safe there, too, I—"

"That's not it. I mean, I have that covered. Or would. Will. In a manner of speaking."

She smiled a little at that. "Good to know."

Oh, but he wanted to consume her, every sweet, smart,

sassy, kind, trusting, wary, innocent, perfect inch of her. "What I meant was that…" He trailed off, realizing there were far more things he wanted to say to her, tell her, than were wise. Especially in a moment like this. "I wanted to…" He kissed her inner thigh, then nudged closer, then kissed her right where it made her hips arch again, made her gasp. "Again," he said. "I'm pretty sure you could, and I rather liked taking you there the first time, so…"

She stopped tugging at his shoulders and gave herself over to his questing tongue. "Seriously?"

He laughed at that. And it felt damn fantastic. He grinned against the inside of her thigh. "Quite, actually."

"Are all Kiwis as…generous as you?" she panted, writhing, as he continued his sweet assault.

"Can't speak for them. Only for myself." He lifted his head, just briefly, to look up at her, so enticing and stunningly beautiful, sprawling naked, waiting for him. She was so responsive, so…perfect. "Are the men of your acquaintance that lacking?"

"Let's just say that a man with your looks and charm isn't generally expected to have a you-first mentality in bed."

"I believe I've been insulted." In response, she sunk her hands into his hair and moved his mouth back where she wanted it. He chuckled…but did as commanded. And when she came again, they both groaned throughout her sweet release.

She reached for him as he pushed himself up farther, until he was lying next to her.

She tucked her leg over his and the entire movement had a familiarity to it that caught at that same part of him that she'd been so effortlessly snagging since he'd busted her foray into a life of crime.

"I was just saying," she said, flushed and still short of breath as she pushed his hair from his face with delicate fingertips, "that if it were normal for men of your ilk to be generous in bed, I wouldn't have been so surprised."

"I have ilk?"

She pushed at him and he responded by rolling her to her back and sliding on top of her. "All I know," he said, "is that making you climax is sexy as bloody hell, and speaking quite selfishly, my ilk and I thoroughly enjoyed the repeat performance."

"You know what I think?" she said, as she shoved his pants down.

He kissed the tip of her nose, shifting off her just long enough to strip the rest of the way down. She was tugging him back before his clothes hit the floor, and he didn't want to be anywhere else. Truly, she was irresistible. "What do you think?"

She shifted under him so she was between his thighs. "I think it's time your ilk stopped talking and started— Oh." She tipped her head back and arched sharply up to meet his first thrust, which filled her perfectly, if the way she held him was any indication. "Right. That."

"Mmm-hmm," he said, smiling as he kissed the side of her neck, and started moving inside her. How she could amuse him and make him so hard it hurt, all at the same time, he had no idea. And, at the moment, didn't much care. Being deep inside Sophie was like sinking into heaven. In fact, he could happily die right then. Well, perhaps a few moments beyond right then. He moved faster…deeper. She urged him to push harder as she dragged her uniform the rest of the way up and over her head.

He slowed when she wriggled to get at her bra. "Stop," he told her, then shifted just enough so he could cover the hard tip of her nipple, straining against the soft pink silk of her bra, with his lips. Her body quivered and he almost lost it right then.

"Simon—"

"Mmm, Sophie," he said, then shifted back up and took her mouth in a deep, fast, hard kiss. A kiss that didn't end, but kept on. And on. As did he. And she met him every thrust of the way. Perfectly.

It was hearing her climb yet again, feeling her tighten further around him, her entire body beginning to shudder beneath him, that drove him straight to the edge.

"Simon," she whispered, then urged his tongue into her mouth, and took him over.

He held on to her as both of their bodies shook with the force of it. He tried to shift his weight off her, but she pulled him straight back down again. "Stay," she asked.

And he did. He didn't want to be anywhere else. Not right then. What came next…he tried not to think about that part.

"What?" she asked, already far more in tune to the subtleties of his body than seemed possible. And yet, didn't he feel the same about hers?

"Nothing." He smiled. "My ilk thanks you. Most intently."

He felt her smile against the side of his neck. "As soon as the world stops spinning and I'm at least somewhat certain I'll regain the use of all my faculties, I'd like to thank your ilk. Personally. And with enormous gratitude."

He was grinning as he slid from her and rolled to his side, taking her with him. She curled into him as if made exclusively for that space. And, just like that, his heart squeezed and thrust him into the next moment, one he was ill prepared for, and, at the moment, defenseless against. That moment where he didn't want to let her go. Where he was forced to acknowledge that he wanted a whole lot more. And not just sex.

"Simon," she said, quietly now, sounding contemplative.

"That was…you are…" He stopped, knowing he sounded like a babbling fool, and not wanting to risk giving voice to even the slightest bit of what he was feeling at that moment.

Later, when he was away from her, and back in his right mind, he'd put this all in perspective. At the moment, he knew he was well and truly compromised, not himself, thinking the crazy thoughts of a man who'd just had the most fabulous, satisfying sex of his life, and was understandably feeling more than was really there.

Which was utter bullshit. He knew what this was, and what this wasn't.

And this wasn't just a quick toss.

He'd known before he'd kissed her that any amount of time spent with Sophie was not going to be enough.

"Don't let reality intrude," she said softly. "Not just yet."

"Would that be so bad?" he said, and realized then he was doomed. He wasn't going to keep quiet, he was going to go down in flames. Idiot.

She lifted her head, looking worried now. "Don't."

"Sophie—"

"Just enjoy this moment, Simon. We both know this can't be about anything else. Well, other than the whole partners in crime part."

"You're out of that. I'll take care of the situation with Tolliver some other way."

She sighed a little, and he felt a bit of the tension leave her body, and not in a good way. "And then what?" She closed her eyes. "Don't answer that."

He brushed a kiss across her lips. "And then we find out what comes next."

"Things that are too good to be true usually are," she said, her voice a whisper now.

He shifted so he could look more directly into her eyes. "Sophie, I want you to know—"

She pushed at him then, and caught him by surprise just enough to wiggle away from him before he could stop her. She slipped off the bed and ducked into the bathroom, shutting the door immediately behind her.

Simon rolled to his back and sighed deeply. Idiot indeed. "Sophie, come back."

She didn't reply. All he heard were some shuffling sounds and a few little grunts. He'd just sat up and swung his legs over the side of the bed, considering if he should go in after her, when the door opened and she stepped out, fully dressed in the clothes he'd first met her in. Her hair was a bit wild, and her cheeks were flushed, but her lips were compressed in a straight, no-nonsense line. And he wanted to part them with his tongue just as badly now as he had before.

"I think I made an error in judgment," she said, and for the first time, he didn't have a quick response. Mostly due to the sudden pressure squeezing his chest. Despite the fact that she had every reason to believe what she'd said, it still hurt to hear the words.

"Not in trying to help you," she quickly added. "I'll always help someone who needs it if I can. I don't think I'm built to look the other way. But…but, even though I really, really wanted to think I could, I'm also not built to just have a fling and enjoy the moment. Much as I wish it were otherwise." She glanced down. "Really, really wish." She looked up again, and her eyes were overly bright. "And even thinking that you might…" She shook her head.

Hurting her was the very last thing he'd want to do. "Sophie, I'm sorry. For a lot of what has happened between us, in regards to the situation I'm involved in. But I won't apologize about what we did here on this bed."

"Maybe if we'd just done it and stayed in the moment. But then you mentioned what comes next and I realized that's exactly how I'm built. To want more, to want it all. And the fantasy was gone and I wanted it for real, and it hurt—a lot, too much for so soon—" She stopped abruptly and looked away, biting her lower lip, which he noted was trembling. Hard.

He reached over the end of the bed and scooped up his own

clothes, quickly slipping on his pants before crossing the room to stand before her. "I understand why you stopped me, even if I wish more than anything you hadn't." He cupped her face, tilted it up to his. "But I had to be honest with you, Sophie. It might not have mattered with someone else. Maybe anyone else. But it matters with you. I do want more. I just haven't a clue how to make that work, and maybe I shouldn't have said anything. But I couldn't just pretend it was meaningless. I didn't want you to think that it was."

She was trembling all over now. He felt horrible. He didn't know what else to say. There were no promises he could make. He could only be honest. "I wish I could just have taken what was there and walked away, happy for the chance to get what I could." He pulled her into his arms, buried his face in her hair. "I guess I'm not made that way, either."

She leaned into him, her cheek pressed against his chest, and all he knew was that he wanted her there. Right there. And the idea of her walking out that door—forever—was completely unacceptable.

And yet, what else could he offer her? As soon as he had the emerald, he was heading home, back across the pond. Her life was here.

"I'm sorry," she whispered, then broke free from his arms and walked to the door of his room.

He took two steps after her, more out of instinct, to stop the feeling like his heart was being ripped from his chest, when she suddenly turned around and walked back to him. And the instinctive, automatic jolt of joy that shot through him was indescribable.

He reached for her, not caring, in that moment, what happened next, just happy it still included her. But she stopped short, ripped the lanyard with her key card over her head and pressed it into his hand. "Use this if you need to. Good luck. I— Goodbye, Simon."

And then she was gone.

11

SOPHIE WHACKED HER ELBOW on the filing cabinet—second time, same spot—and swore under her breath as she made her way back to her desk. She tried to ignore the new lanyard and key tag swinging from her neck…and the memories that went with it.

Two days. That was how much time she'd given him. She'd burned two sick days, holed up in her apartment, and spent way too much time thinking about Simon Lassiter. But she'd spoken about him to no one. Not even Delia, though that hadn't exactly been a problem. Her friend had spent every waking moment that they'd been in contact since Sophie had called after leaving Simon's room talking about her own problems, which, to be fair, weren't small. The wedding was still on and mere days away. But all was not well in Wingate Wedding World.

Sophie had mumbled something about food poisoning and being too sick to even answer her phone or come to the door, and apologized for worrying her friend that day and for not being able to retrieve her phone. She'd explained about it being the wrong room, but by then Delia had been off and running, alternately ranting and sobbing about her situation, leaving Sophie to mercifully keep the rest of the truth to herself.

Two days. Not one word from Simon. And far too many words from Delia. Nothing seemed the same. And yet everything was exactly how it always was. Even Delia's breakdowns weren't all that unusual, as dealing with the Wingate family had never been exactly easy. Now there was increased tension between her and Adam, who had become suspicious when his call to Delia's phone—which, it turned out, had mercifully died at some point during the night—had gone straight to voice mail, and had badgered her about why it wasn't plugged in and why she hadn't called him back when she'd realized it wasn't on and she'd missed his daily call.

Perhaps he'd sensed something was amiss, although it took very little, real or perceived, for Adam to flip out, or perhaps it was Delia's guilty conscience prodding her, but, in the end, she'd confessed to him about the stealth bachelorette party, which had put Sophie squarely on Adam's shit list, or at least higher on it than she'd been before, and claimed that she'd left her phone in the pub. Which, as it turned out, was the truth. Just not the pub they'd actually started the evening in. And, of course, she'd managed to conveniently leave all the parts of what had come directly after, and with whom, out of her confession. Which was why there was still a wedding on Sunday.

Which meant, everything that had happened, all of it…for nothing. If only Delia had remembered where she'd left her phone in the first place, none of it would have taken place.

And Sophie wouldn't have spent the past two days seesawing back and forth over whether she wished she'd known sooner…or preferred that things had happened exactly as they had.

But, as for Adam and Delia, she was convinced that if it hadn't been the missed phone call, and the subsequent confession about the bachelorette party setting him off, it would have been something else. A truth Sophie had tried, once again, to gently point out to her friend, but Delia was so upset over his cool attitude toward her since their most recent blowout, and his subtle threats to call the wedding off if she didn't "behave more intelligently," that she wasn't in the right frame of mind to listen to Sophie. Sophie knew exactly what she'd like to do to Adam, and his condescending attitude and super controlling demands, but Delia wasn't interested in her vengeance scenarios, either.

Of course, there was that part where Delia had actually done something much worse than attend an un-Wingate-sanctioned bachelorette party, but given how Sophie had spent that twenty-four hour period, and with whom, she was more than willing to pretend that entire little scenario had never happened if Delia was.

So...Sophie had gone back to life as usual. Listening to her friend sob and rail, working her shifts, collapsing during her off hours. She would have thought the wedding prep chaos and the increased media and guest events surrounding the upcoming Art Institute gala would have preoccupied her to the point of not thinking about Simon every second of the day. All it had done was exhaust her already exhausted self, who was not sleeping worth a damn, despite her intense fatigue. And she thought about him. Constantly.

Matters weren't helped any by Adam's mother, who was still ranting every chance she got—which was hourly—about how she couldn't believe that the museum had the nerve not to change the date of their annual gala when the wedding date had been announced. The museum had informed her the first time she'd thrown a fit that they scheduled their events several years in advance, in order to secure the loaned collections from their donors. But then, a little thing like logic had never stopped Arlene Wingate before, and it sure as hell wasn't going to stop her now.

Which meant a daily tug-of-war between Arlene and Sven, the gala coordinator—who had many guests booked into the Wingate—with the hotel managers square in the middle.

Probably because of the heightened stress level of the entire hotel staff, security hadn't even given her much grief over having to replace her key tag. She'd been almost nauseous enough when she'd approached their office, terrified that her activities would somehow be revealed, that faking a food poisoning incident as her reason for leaving her key tag in a restaurant and not realizing she'd lost it until reporting for work two days later was a relative breeze.

All that stomach-churning terror, and all she'd gotten was the standardized lecture about the vital nature of safety and security for the hotel and all its guests, then was sternly informed by her immediate supervisor that given her exemplary work history, she wouldn't be written up this time, but that another infraction would result in a report being put in her file and a possible demotion or dismissal. Otherwise, it was have a nice day, and don't eat the shellfish.

Normal. All back to normal.

So why didn't she feel back to normal? Sure, it had only been a few days, and the entire episode with Simon wasn't exactly a forgettable way to spend a day, but it was more than that. She worried. Not about the key tag, or what he might have done with it. No, that would be normal. What did she worry about? What had made the past two nights the longest of her life? Wondering if he was okay. Had she given him enough time with the key before the replacement had rendered his tag invalid? Had he recovered the velvet box and whatever was inside? Was he, right now, on his way back to England, gone from the hotel, and her life, forever? Was Tolliver hot on his heels, or had he accepted the loss of the object, knowing it was never his to begin with?

Did Simon miss her?

She missed him. She couldn't even pretend to claim otherwise. She rolled her chair forward and stared, sightlessly, at the files on her desk. She had a pile of work to do. Being gone two nights straight had left an overstuffed inbox and dozens of calls to return. She wondered how the day managers handled the job, when her far more narrow field of responsibility covering the night hours seemed so chaotic and unwieldy. There was only so much a manager could take responsibility for from midnight to six, though it had its share of special concerns. Mostly in the form of noise control, overly exuberant parties, late arrivals who hadn't confirmed, inebriated guests, unwelcome visitors, that sort of thing.

But the guests were a lot more demanding during regular business hours. Most of the time on her watch, the guests were asleep. It was only the ones who weren't who could make her life interesting. Of course, day management was her goal. It was the next step.

She propped an elbow on her desk and rested her forehead in her palm as she sorted through the latest stack of reports from security, must-return call slips, urgent notices from the kitchen and the front desk and the housecleaning staff. At that moment, the idea of taking on a hotel of the size of the Wingate seemed like a career path only an insane person would choose. "A life of crime seems much less intense."

One thing she hadn't done was check up on the occupancy of a certain room…or a certain suite. The less she knew about Simon's whereabouts, and Tolliver's, likely the best for them all. Or, that's what she told herself. But it had taken almost superhuman control to resist even a peek.

Her door burst open, and Mick, the concierge, popped his head in. "I have a problem."

Her entire body tensed. This was what she'd feared, every waking moment, since leaving Simon's room. The moment the hotel would discover a crime had occurred. "Of course you do," she responded, lifting her head, heart pounding. She forced a smile. "Which is why we hired you. Because you're a problem solver. It's in the job description. And you're very good at your job."

"Yes. Well, this time the guest in question wants to speak to you. And only you."

She couldn't help it, her heart skipped a beat. What other guest would want to speak to her and her alone? Was this Simon's way of contacting her through business channels, to make their connection appear legit? And why in the hell was she even wondering that, since she'd decided to walk away? She would hardly go back just because he'd crooked his little finger.

Visions of all parts of Simon, crooked and otherwise, filled her already vision-filled brain. She crossed her ankles and pressed them together against the urge to get up and run.

The question was, which way would she have run?

Then another thought struck her. What if it was Tolliver waiting impatiently to speak with her? What if he'd noticed something missing and was making good on his threat to contact management and security? What if he noticed that she was the maid from the other day? Simon had said he was far more observant than he let on.

Now her legs began to tremble, but not in a pleasurable-memory-induced kind of way.

"Who is it," she asked, trying to keep the internal quaking out of the tone of her voice, "and what does it pertain to?"

"One of our guests is putting something of great value—according to him—in our hotel safe, and he wants to post his own security personnel. Our security is understandably not enthusiastic about the idea, and…this has led to a demand to speak with the manager." Mick, who was always meticulously groomed with never so much as a plucked eyebrow out of place, always managed to somehow maintain himself as the calm in the center of any storm, no matter the size. Behind closed doors, however, he was quite the animated gossip. It was for both of those reasons that he was one of Sophie's favorite people.

He managed an apologetic smile. "That would be you,

darling. I tried to mediate the best I could, but, my dearest innocent, if you could see the size of those behemoths Mr. Tolliver wants to post—"

Everything past the name "Tolliver" landed on deaf ears. The fact that he was wanting to deposit something into the safe meant that Simon hadn't retrieved anything yet, because what were the chances he had some other priceless piece he wanted to stash?

She had prayed that whenever whatever shit was going to hit the fan, indeed did hit the fan, that it would happen on the day shift. She supposed it was karmic justice that it was happening at night, during her shift. It didn't mean she had to like it.

"What, exactly, is the beef?" she asked, feeling the complete lack of sleep for the past three days taking its toll all at once.

"The key word there being 'beef,' believe you me. Mr. Tolliver wants to post private security in the form of two men the size of the Roman Coliseum in the general vicinity of the hotel safe. Now, if only they could be persuaded to wear togas, I might be more enthusiastic about the endeavor, but—"

"And what, precisely, does he want these two pillars of Rome to do?"

"Observe anyone going in and out of the safe, and make certain that no one enters the safe that hasn't followed protocol with the front-desk security."

Which was why her security guys were pissed. Men, in general, didn't like to be made to feel as if they were inadequate at...well, anything. But they especially didn't like their supposed vulnerabilities exposed in such a public and emasculating way. "They cannot interact with the guests, and they cannot impede the entrance or exit of anyone into the safe. If there are any concerns, whatsoever, in that regard, they can report either to their boss, who can contact security or the manager on duty, or they can simply report to either of those resources directly." Mick started to interrupt, but she lifted her hand to stall him. "If, at any time, those rules are not followed, Mr. Tolliver's security detail will be detained immediately by security and turned over to the local authorities, if whatever infractions they committed are deemed necessary of that particular treatment, and Mr. Tolliver will be asked to remove his valuables from the safe and check out immediately."

"But—"

"Please relay that message to both Mr. Tolliver and security, the latter of which is free to contact me directly. I'm sure Mr. Tolliver will be tolerant of my concerns in this manner, especially as he's getting, more or less, what he's asked for." She looked back down at her work, thankful her concierge couldn't see the way her legs still shook under her desk.

Mick just stood in the doorway, staring, until she looked up again.

"Is there anything else?"

He sighed. "You know, some days I hate my job."

She smiled wearily. "Join the club. And, Mick," she said, calling him back when he resolutely turned to leave. "I'm sorry you're stuck in this situation. I understand Mr. Tolliver can be something of a tyrant, and we both know what security can be like. I don't envy you, but I'd appreciate it if you could make this go away. I'm really rather deep in the swamp here." She motioned to the stacks on her desk.

Mick smiled at her. "I'll do my best for you, my sweet."

"I know you will. And I'll owe you."

He winked. "Oh, and I'll collect."

She smiled back, and waited until he'd closed the door to do a face-plant on her desk. She groaned, then drummed her feet hard on the floor. Neither made her feel particularly better.

What would make her feel better—much, much better— was to see Simon again.

No. No, no, no, no. That would be bad, she schooled herself. On a Delia-impulsive-decision-making level of bad. She'd done the smart thing. She'd realized she was in over her head, in more ways than one, and she'd immediately extricated herself from the situation. If her life was a movie, surely the women in the audience would be cheering her smart heroine behavior in that moment.

Either that, or rooting for her and the sexy, handsome New Zealander to somehow make things work out.

"Seriously. No more afternoon movies on Lifetime for you."

She forced herself upright, but there was no way she was going to be able to concentrate on a single detail on her desk until she found out how things had shaken down with Tolliver and security. And with the velvet box presumably in the hotel safe, she couldn't help but wonder what Simon's plans would be now. Not that she could in any way involve herself. To do so not only put herself at risk, but could also put Simon in harm's way. Something had prodded Tolliver to use the hotel safe. Simon said he was paranoid and a control freak—hence the henchmen on hotel safe duty—but she doubted he'd just suddenly decided to do that after initially choosing to keep it with him at all times.

She stiffened. What if Tolliver had caught Simon trying to steal—retrieve—it? What if, right now, Simon was in some kind of trouble? Security hadn't been alerted to any potential thefts, and the last time the cops had been called was last week with that frat party fiasco. She might have been home for the past two shifts, but had anything happened on that level, she'd have known within five minutes of reporting for work.

So she forced her brain to stop the roller-coaster ride it was about to embark on, before it left the launch pad and picked up too much speed. She was out of the Simon-Tolliver situation, professionally and personally. Well, other than her moral obligation to the hotel as an employee. As a manager, she was supposed to be vigilant if any news came to her attention regarding a potential problem that could arise between a guest and the staff, or a guest and another guest, and take immediate action if deemed necessary.

Of course, she'd also learned in her college hotel management courses that effective, successful managers were creative in solving problems, using whatever tools they might have at their disposal to rectify a potential crisis as swiftly and cleanly as possible, mitigating potential fallout to the best of their ability.

And hadn't that been what she was doing, helping Simon retrieve an item that did not rightfully belong to another guest? She'd used her key tag in a professional, if slightly rule-bending manner, and done her best to assess the situation and resolve it in a way that would lessen the possibility of greater damage if left in the hands of the guests.

Which was so much bullshit, but it made her feel better, at least momentarily, to think of it that way. Yes, she'd failed, much as she'd failed in her attempt to help Delia. Clearly, a life of criminal behavior was not something she should pursue any further. But she'd been trying. Truly. Trying to mitigate fallout between Delia and Adam, and the rest of the Wingate clan. Trying to mitigate the chances of Simon and Tolliver coming to blows, or worse, if he'd tried to retrieve the velvet case. If she'd been successful in either endeavor, her best friend wouldn't be so miserable, and Simon could be on a plane back to England, leaving Tolliver to handle his loss—hopefully—privately.

Instead, Delia was an emotional wreck, so different now from the woman she'd been when the two had become friends, that Sophie was truly worried for her as she approached what should have been the happiest day of her life, and Simon was possibly even further away from achieving his goal of righting a wrong and restoring a family heirloom to its rightful owner. And, somehow, Tolliver had been alerted to the fact that something wasn't entirely kosher with his current plan of security, which meant he wasn't a happy Wingate guest. And an unhappy guest was a potential problem guest. And someone of Tolliver's magnitude could prove quite problematic.

So much for her mitigation skills.

She shoved back from her desk and got up to pace. She hated being stuck in here, not knowing what was going on, but didn't dare show her face until she was certain Tolliver was tucked safely back in his suite. She briefly debated heading over to security to watch the monitors and see for herself what was happening at the safe, as well as take a peek at any activity in the hallway outside Tolliver's rooms. She could use the recent contretemps as her excuse to enter security's inner sanctum, but that would still mean dealing with them and listening to their litany of all the reasons why guests should not interfere with hotel security staff.

She wouldn't be at all surprised if they waited for the day shift to start and took up their argument again with the general manager, who was several decades Sophie's senior, professionally and chronologically. It was likely they'd win the argument, but by then she'd be at home, and out of the direct line of sight of Tolliver, when the issue was resolved one way or the other. She might get a call, or a command performance to come in early tomorrow for a meeting with her supervisor to discuss her decision, but that still kept her out of Tolliver's direct path.

There was another knock on her door, making her jump, but she took a breath and reflexively smoothed a hand over her shirt before responding. "Come in."

Mick stuck his head in the door, then realized she was standing away from her desk and swung the door open wider.

Sophie slid a step to her right so as not to be seen through the open doorway. "And?"

"Tolliver is mollified, security is livid. I heard them discussing taking the matter to Gretchen in the morning."

Gretchen was the general manager, known privately amongst the rest of the staff as Frau Dourface.

"I'm sorry," he added.

"That's okay, I assumed as much. At least it's under control for now."

"Also, Delia asked me to tell you she was going to drop in after she closes De Trop." He leaned farther into the room and whispered, "Our darling bride-to-be appears quite distressed."

Sophie swallowed a sigh of her own. As worried about Delia as she was, she really wasn't up to dealing with her best friend's latest round of concerns, but it beat dealing directly with Tolliver, and it would get her mind off Simon, and where he was at that exact moment. And what he was doing. What he was thinking. And were any of his thoughts about her.

"Yes, well, the wedding is this weekend and things are not lovely in lovebird land."

"So I hear." He glanced over his shoulder and stepped a bit more into the room. "But, frankly, not all that surprised."

Mick was one of the best concierges in Chicago for a reason. He was discreet, he was dedicated, and he knew when to reach out, and when to take care of business on his own so the hotel remained above any less-than-legitimate dealings when it came to making their guests happy. She knew Mick was loyal to the Wingates, but that his concern for Delia was sincere, and that anything said here would remain between them.

"Why do you say that?" Sophie asked. Not that it was a big secret that things between Delia and Adam were rather… tense. But that was something only the Wingate family, and the closest of hotel employees, knew. To the public, and more importantly, the media, they were still the Cinderella couple. The wedding was marketing gold for the hotel magnate family and they weren't about to let a minor internal squabble get in the way of all the free publicity raining down on the happy couple, and, hence, the hotel itself.

But she wanted to know what Mick was thinking, which was a reflection of what the staff was thinking. Just hopefully not saying. Every employee had to sign a confidentiality agreement as per course of employment, but this was the biggest event to happen in the history of the Chicago Wingate, and she knew the media and tabloids were waving around significant sums, sniffing for anything they could exploit for higher circulation numbers. So far, no one had caved, but that was mostly due to the public face Delia was putting on her private pain.

Mick glanced over his shoulder again, then looked back to Sophie. "Of course, everyone knows what a controlling, egomaniacal bitch Adam can be. Remember, those of us who have been here for a while had to deal with him as general manager back when Daddy Wingate made him earn his stripes the hard way. Trust me, those days will never be forgotten. Gretchen is like Glinda the Good Witch, comparatively."

Hard as that was to believe but Sophie had heard the stories. More and more of them since Adam had taken up with Delia.

"We were all stunned when he started his relationship with Delia," Mick went on. "He'd never once dated outside his trust fund pool before, much less anyone his family wouldn't approve of. We thought it was a short-term rebellion kind of thing, but then it seemed to grow legs and we began to harbor hopes that our sweet Miss Delia would be the one to smooth out his, shall we say, less than generous edges."

"And what is the general consensus now?"

"That whatever reason he got together with her—and who knows, maybe he really did care for her at some point—his family has gotten too intrusive, *quelle surprise,* and, well, once a controlling son of a bitch, always a controlling son of a bitch. If it's between making Delia happy, or making Mommy Dearest happy, we all know where his fealty lies. We all feel sorry for her. She's a shadow of the happy girl we knew and loved. I just wish there was something I could do to help her defend herself better. I appreciate the Wingates, they've been very good to me, but it's no secret they can be barracudas. It's what got them to the top of their food chain. I'm just afraid our Delia hasn't grown a tough enough skin to handle the constant nipping."

Sophie nodded. "I know, and I worry, too, Mick." She was relieved that his concerns were still the general ones they'd all expressed to Delia, in some way or another, as her relationship with Adam had progressed and the engagement was announced. Apparently, and thank God, word hadn't gotten out about her friend's unplanned drunken sleepover with a hotel guest. Mick would have been discreet in making Sophie aware of any rumors, but he'd have made it known to her, if, for no other reason, so she could protect her friend. "You're a good friend, Mick. I'll let her know you're there for her. She can use all the support she can get."

He nodded and started to back out the door, then paused. "It's a shame, you know, that there isn't any way to end the engagement without destroying herself professionally, or even socially."

Sophie eyed the concierge and wondered just what he knew about that night, but he hadn't spoken of it and Sophie certainly wouldn't question him. It was the thing about him she loved. And she knew, without doubt, he would have protected her just the same. "With the wedding less than a week away?" Sophie snorted. "Can you imagine the Wingates' reaction to that?"

Mick shuddered. "A nightmare of epic proportions."

The real shame, Sophie thought, was that the Wingates didn't even want Delia as a member of the family. But once they'd thrown the entire weight of their legacy behind the wedding of the year, there was no way to gracefully withdraw.

"Tell her I'm in my office trying to catch up unless dragged out by the evil forces of hotel management. She can come over whenever she gets done working."

"I'll pass the word." He smiled. "You really do need to take a gander at the pillars of steel when you get the chance. It's quite the visual feast."

"I'll girder my strength and treat myself later. Back to your post, you, before the hotel collapses without your vigilant caretaking."

"And it would, too," he said, as he closed the door behind him.

"Probably," Sophie murmured, sitting once again at her desk, and picking up the phone slips and urgent messages.

IT WAS CLOSE TO THREE in the morning by the time she'd plowed through the worst of it. She glanced at the clock, debating another cup of coffee. Her shift ended at six and she relished nothing more at the moment then the thought of going home and trying to sleep until her next shift, but Delia had called an hour earlier, saying she was delayed with some staffing issues that she needed to handle after the club closed, and would be over to see her when she got done, that she "really needed to talk."

Sophie sighed and got up to get another cup of coffee. Chances were she wasn't going to get much sleep anyway. Delia had sounded...determined. Which was new, at least. Sophie snagged a few pieces of wrapped chocolate from the dish next to the coffeepot. Reinforcements were never a bad idea.

She'd barely sat down when Delia rapped once and stuck her head in the door. "Good time?"

Sophie motioned her in.

Her friend was, in more ways than just in personality, the

exact opposite of Sophie. She was lean and trim, where Sophie was soft and curvy. She was tanned and blonde, where Sophie was red curls and freckles. She was tall and leggy, where Sophie was…not. Unless by leggy you meant she had strong English peasant stock running through her gene pool. Which was all to say she'd do better harvesting potatoes than walking the runway. Delia was also impulsive, endlessly optimistic, bubbly with a ready laugh, and had a much sharper mind than her Barbie doll appearance might suggest. Except when it came to Adam.

Sophie was as an optimist, too, but perhaps one with a slightly more realistic outlook. She was a thinker, whereas Delia was a leaper. Which was why Sophie took a cautious breath, then popped another chocolate as her best friend paced inside her office.

"So," Sophie started, "you sounded like you'd made some decisions. Did the staffing situation work itself out?"

"What? Oh, that. No, but it will. I had to fire one of my hostesses for fraternizing with one of the guests—"

Sophie raised her eyebrows at that, given Delia's own fraternizing situation, but Delia waved it away. "If she'd been discreet, I'd have just had a talk with her, but she was on duty at the time. And it was in the club. And she was in his lap."

"Ah."

"Right. That led to the discovery that a couple of the girls actually had a little side business going, leading some of our more…successful guests to believe there was perhaps more to be had at De Trop than drinks and dancing."

"Wow."

"Well, I didn't have hard proof, or I'd have had them all arrested. I don't think it was that well organized, but I had enough to fire them without references. Nobody said a word about unfair business practices, which leads me to believe I had it all right. And if I missed anybody, I'm sure they'll think twice about continuing with their side gig."

"Sounds like an eventful night."

Delia finally flopped down in the seat facing Sophie's desk. "It was a distraction and I could use a few of those right about now."

"Really? Because I'd think the Wingates would be distraction enough right about now."

"Distraction *from* the Wingates," she clarified.

And Sophie totally understood that. Wasn't she planning to sleep away her free time just to keep from thinking about Simon?

Delia slumped a little in her seat. "I'm not sure I can hold up until the weekend, Soph."

"You sounded, I don't know...energized, when you called, like maybe you'd come to some kind of conclusion about something?"

Delia sighed and gave Sophie a look that said, don't start. But it was too late for that.

"I know, I know, we've been over it all before and you know how I feel," Sophie reassured her. "I'm not going to hammer you with my opinion. Not tonight, anyway."

"Good, because no way am I calling off the wedding."

"Can I just ask you...given what's gone on the past few days, and Adam's attitude toward you, are you not calling it off because you're still in love and want to marry this man? Or are you not calling it off because you're afraid the powerful Wingate machine would crush you up and spit you out if you so much as tried?" She lifted a hand before Delia could respond. "Maybe I should put it this way. If you could have anything you wanted with no repercussions, as far as your future with Adam, would you still want to marry him this weekend, or would you prefer more time to figure things out?"

"That's a moot question because there will be repercussions for any action I take."

Sophie softened her tone. "Is that why you're not taking any?"

Delia gazed down at her hands and fiddled with the serious diamond adorning her ring finger.

"Del, do you love him? Really love him? Because, Wingate family and your career aside, he's the one you have to spend your life with."

Finally Delia looked at her friend, and Sophie hated the resignation she found there. "Do any of us know what we really want, Soph? Adam is a catch a dozen times over."

"If you're talking financial security and appearance, yes, he is that. But what about the rest? What about—"

"Maybe I don't care as much about the rest as everyone else seems to."

"You forget, I've known you a long time. Of course you care about the rest. It's why you didn't settle for that ass of an investment banker you went out with two years ago, who was supposedly the catch of the century and showered you with expensive gifts and fabulous dates, but could only be bothered to actually listen to you when he wasn't umbilically attached to his BlackBerry, which was always. You're smart, Delia, and you can take care of your own finances. You need someone who is a match for who you are, not—"

"I thought we weren't going to have this discussion?" she said dryly. "Again." She straightened in her seat. "The wedding is this Sunday. It's now Wednesday. Well, Thursday, actually. Let's be realistic here. It's not going to get called off."

"So, what were you sounding so determined about when you called me?"

"Well, maybe what you've said has had more of an impact on me than you realized. Or maybe he's just been hard enough on me this week that I'm thinking about things a little differently—"

"Delia—"

"So, first, I made myself consider the worst-case scenario."

"Which is?" Sophie asked warily.

"We marry, I decide it really isn't the best thing for me, and I file for divorce. I signed a prenup, so there won't be any talk that I married him for the money, and, sure, I'll have to start over somewhere else as I'm not exactly going to be hired to work here again—"

"You agreed to a prenup? When did that happen?"

Delia glanced at her hands again. "Monday. You were still out sick. And, I knew you'd give me a hard time about it, but—"

"I understand his family is richer than Croesus, but if he really loves you—"

"He does love me, Sophie. You all pick on him, but he's under a ton of pressure. It's not easy being a Wingate, especially the only son. And, though they're a tough bunch, we all benefit from that. I mean, our livelihoods are directly a result of their toughness, their success, so we shouldn't be so quick to spurn—"

"You've been assimilated after all."

"You know," Delia said, fire in her voice for the first time that night, "you could be a little more grateful."

"Me? What did I do?"

"You criticize the Wingate family all the time, but you draw a paycheck from them."

"Because I do a damn good job. A job I'm dedicated to and work my ass off for. The Wingates will never find fault with my ability to do my job or my focus to that job. But it's a job, Delia. I'm an employee, not a member of the family. And it's not Wingate Hotel I have any issues with. I am treated well here and I like the challenge. But when the family who happens to own this hotel starts treating my best friend like something someone scrapes off the bottom of their shoe, you better believe I'm going to speak up."

"And you don't find that hypocritical?"

"Do you honestly believe that it is?"

"I'm just saying that you're nipping at the hand that feeds you."

"If I had issues with how they operate their hotel, then yes, it would be unfair of me to bitch but not say or do anything about it, yet still draw a paycheck. But I don't have to personally like the owner of my company in order to feel okay being employed by the company." She sat back and took a breath. Maybe she shouldn't have had that caffeine after all. "And just how on earth did this become about me?" Then something Delia had said struck a chord. "Wait. Back up a minute. What did you say before, about getting rehired here if you filed for divorce?"

Suddenly Delia was fascinated with her hands again.

"Dee?"

"What? I just meant I wouldn't be working for the Wingate empire if I divorced a Wingate."

"You said rehired. Not fired. If you divorced Adam, the consensus is they'd fire you from your job." Delia didn't look up. "Spill the rest."

"Well, after Adam found out about the bachelorette party, he confided in me that his sisters have been pressuring him about my work here."

"He 'confided' in you?"

She looked up then, and even though her chin was up, her lips were a bit quavery, and Sophie immediately felt like a complete heel for pushing at her friend. She just hated to see her hurt, and hated even more if she was contributing to the misery.

"He just explained, again, that being a Wingate wife would bring with it a ton of new responsibilities and he'd be honored—honored, Sophie, his word—if I'd agree to step down from my manager's job and devote myself to helping him."

"As in, working for him?"

"Not employed no, but as his wife, I'm an important asset and I want to be available to—"

"Do you? I mean, it's okay if you do, Dee, I'm just— You worked hard to get where you are so I am sincerely asking. Are you okay with giving up your career to help him with his?"

"That's the decision I made. That's what I came to tell you. I want us to be a unit, a team, so I need to see us that way, think about us that way. It's no longer me versus him, or my career versus his. We're going to be an us, Soph. And if this helps foster that unified front, then yes, I'll gladly shift my focus. I can always go back to work if it turns out I don't feel I'm fulfilling my personal potential."

Privately, Sophie had her doubts about that. Not as long as Dee remained a Wingate, anyway. And though Adam might need a full-time hostess as a wife, Sophie suspected there was more to it than that. It wouldn't surprise her in the least if Adam's sisters were concerned about having to introduce their future sister-in-law as a nightclub manager. Even if it was a premiere club in their own damn hotel. That wasn't something a Wingate did. It was something they hired others to do. Delia did it very well. But that wouldn't be good enough.

"I just want you to be happy, Dee. I know you and Adam have had this whirlwind romance, and maybe it is all the pressures of his family that are making him be a bit more… tense with you lately."

"I didn't agree to give up managing De Trop just because I was trying to smooth things over after the party debacle. But I do think it will go a long way toward unifying me with him, which, in turn, will help solidify my standing with the family."

Sophie didn't say anything immediately.

"I do think we can be happy, Sophie. Wingate fallout or not, I wouldn't marry him if I didn't think we had a shot."

She nodded, and tried to bite her tongue, but with the rehearsal and the dinners, and the rest of the prewedding events swinging into full gear Friday, this might be the last chance they had to talk privately. She took a breath and just said it. "I know we haven't talked about it, but what happened the other night—"

"Was a mistake, Sophie. I was drunk and I was scared. It'll never happen again. If Adam and I don't make it, then I'll end things with him. I wouldn't cheat on him."

Sophie nodded again. "I know. But..." She looked at her friend, and there was no censure in her tone now, just a sincere expression of concern. "I'm sorry I've been hard on you. It's just that I care about you more than anyone and I hate seeing you get hurt. I worry that you're caught in the middle, and I—I just wish you were happier going into this."

"I am happier now that I've decided what path to take. I think it's just that the wedding has become this huge media event. It's not about our getting married anymore. He's just not handling it really well." She leaned forward. "But, even with all the craziness and the pressure, he still wants to marry me, Soph. He loves me."

Sophie wondered how much Adam was caught in the middle, too, but she kept that to herself. Delia was clearly committed to making a go of it, so it was time to stop cautioning her and start supporting her friend's decision. Besides, given her behavior over the past few days, who was she to talk about making wise choices where men were concerned?

"Okay."

"Okay?" her friend asked warily.

Sophie smiled and leaned forward to extend both hands to her best friend. "Okay. Let's get ready for a wedding!"

Delia beamed and put her hands in Sophie's and squeezed tight. "It's all going to work out, Sophie. You'll see."

Sophie squeezed back. And, incongruously, her thoughts shot to Simon. And how close she had come to making a really bad choice with him. And how, even now, she wasn't sure she'd done the right thing. "I want it to work out, Dee. More than anything, I want you to be happy."

But after they'd shared hugs and Delia had gone, Sophie was still left sitting there, realizing that she'd been saying the words to Dee, and meaning them, but in her heart, she'd also been thinking them about herself.

12

SIMON PACED. TWO DAYS. Two pointless, fruitless days. He'd spent that time shadowing Tolliver and his "business associate" as he'd overheard him introduce his beaming brunette shower buddy at a lunch meeting with a member of the press earlier that day. Or yesterday, as the case may be. He didn't bother glancing at the illuminated clock dial beside his bed. He knew it was well into the wee hours. He also knew from the past two nights that sleep was a commodity his restless brain wasn't prepared to allow his exhausted body to have. Not until he had that damned emerald in his grasp. Or at least a solid game plan on how to get it.

And now that game plan was going to be even harder to come by.

"Why the shift to the safe?" he muttered for at least the hundredth time. And, for the hundredth time, he had no immediate answer. Simon had been careful to stay well hidden, well disguised, as he'd tailed his former employer. No way had Tolliver made him. But, who knows, maybe he'd felt the surveillance. Given his notorious paranoia, it wasn't entirely out of character to make the sudden change, and the reason could be something only Tolliver would think suspicious. The old man was also supremely wary of anyone who wasn't in his direct employ, which was why he had his own team on premises at the Art Institute, watching over the collection as it was being installed. He'd probably babysit it himself if he thought he could handle any potential threat.

Whatever Tolliver's reasons, the fact remained that there were now two very beefy sentries posted by the entrance to the hotel safety-deposit boxes. Which meant the gemstone wouldn't make an appearance until the night of the gala. Where it would be spotlighted around the neck of his "business associate." Why the pretense there, Simon had no clue. Tolliver's wife had passed on decades before, and though his personal life wasn't tabloid news, it wasn't any secret that he enjoyed the company of much younger, very beautiful women, whose only business appeared to be keeping the egos of older, wealthier men amply inflated. Perhaps it was the prestige of the benefit-oriented event that demanded he appear somewhat more interested in raising money than chasing women who were, at best, a third his age.

Simon tried to recall the time when he'd been under the magnetic spell Tolliver could so effortlessly weave when it moved him. He'd convinced Simon that philanthropy was his passion, and that restoring his personal heritage was important to him, as a means of settling, once and for all, a generations-old feud, so he could return his full attention to the business of helping others. Simon had fully believed while executing his mission that the documentation Tolliver had "uncovered" was authentic, despite meeting Guinn, whom he'd genuinely liked and respected, and whom his gut had told him was the one to be believed.

Now, Simon knew too much about the real Tolliver, the "man behind the curtain" as it were, about where his narrow-viewed, spiteful passions really lay, to ever imagine being swayed by his once powerful rhetoric again. But Simon had watched the poor sap interviewing his former boss and mentor leave lunch with his face almost glowing from the golden light that was Tolliver's charm and magnetism.

He couldn't let him get away with this. Not only for Guinn's sake, but because it simply wasn't right.

Simon needed a plan.

He needed Sophie.

He rubbed his hands over his face. And this time it had nothing to do with her key card. He wanted her here because he missed her. Because she had a sharp mind that he could bounce ideas off of. Because she respected what he was trying to do, and would help him figure out a solution, even if the solution couldn't involve her directly.

She understood him in a way no one else seemed to, maybe in ways even he didn't fully comprehend. She had a different perspective on things than he did, came at them from a different angle, but it was one he always understood when he listened to her. She made sense to him. That was the only way he could think to describe how he felt about her. Everything about her just made sense to him.

But that was one option that was not open to him. *So, stop thinking about her and start thinking about how you're going to get that damn stone off that skinny supermodel's neck.* Tolliver would likely have guard dogs shadowing him at the gala, just as he likely wouldn't let his date for the event so much as separate herself more than a few inches from him all night. The only time he could see where she'd be given any tether was to go to the loo, and even then, Tolliver would send someone with her. No way would he let her wander off with that piece of history around her neck.

Simon shoved off the bed and jerked open the door to the mini fridge, stared at the same overpriced, less than appetizing selections he had the last time he'd done this, and slapped the door shut again, empty-handed.

He paced. He downed half a bottle of water. He paced some more, then finally groaned and did a spread-eagle face-plant on the bed. Was it pathetic that he couldn't stop thinking about her? Or that he was spending as much time trying to come up with some wild-ass game plan that would get her back into his life as he was trying to find a solution to the Tolliver problem? He didn't even try to fool himself into thinking he needed her to get the job done. No, this was about him needing her for himself. It was about her being irreplaceable to him. Personally.

He didn't do personally. His lifestyle didn't really permit a personally. And, if and when he decided to somehow fit a personally into his life, it would certainly have to be with someone who could actually factor into his day-to-day life. Not someone a continent away.

"Someone who hasn't already walked out on you would also be a good place to start," he muttered. He was contemplating taking a reviving shower, ordering from the room service menu, or pulling a pillow over his face and attempting to get some much needed sleep, when there was a light tap on his door.

"Housekeeping," someone said quietly.

His heart stopped, then started up again in double time. He cautioned himself to slow down, think, before reacting any further. He rolled his head and looked at the clock. It was just after six in the morning. Good God, another whole night without sleep.

Guardedly, with an almost sickening rush of adrenaline pulsing into his exhausted system, he rolled off the bed to his feet, and cautiously approached the door to the hallway. He believed Tolliver wasn't remotely aware that he'd trailed him to Chicago. But something had made him decide to use the hotel safe. If the quiet voice on the other side of that door belonged to anyone over six foot with a jacket size of forty-four or more, he was in for some unpleasant company.

He palmed his gun from his ankle strap and positioned

himself, back to the wall next to the doorknob side of the door. And waited.

A nerve-racking minute later, there was another whisper-light tap. "Housekeeping."

Either the hulking security agent on the other side of the door had a remarkably girly voice, or there was no hulking security agent. He did a quick visual scan through the peephole. Short, female, head bowed, hairnet, maid's uniform. His heart was skipping all kinds of crazy beats, but he schooled himself to remain calm. Despite the fact that there could only be one maid in this entire hotel who would be standing outside his door at 6:00 am.

"It's six in the morning," he said quietly, so his voice would reach just past the door, but no further. "What could I possibly need from housekeeping?"

"Me."

He flipped the locks off the door, pulled it open, tugged the maid in his room, closed the door behind her, then pushed her up against it. "Really? And why is that?"

He pulled off the dark hairnet and soft strawberry curls came tumbling out. His heart tumbled right along with them.

Sophie looked up at him. "Tolliver is suddenly using the hotel safe. I tried to keep my distance. I shouldn't be here. I should steer clear of this whole thing, and most especially you."

"But?"

She searched his face. "But I had to know if you were okay."

"Sophie…" It was exactly what he wanted. Her, back in his arms, back in his life. Nothing else seemed more paramount than that. At that moment, he didn't give a rat's ass about the job or what she could do to help him.

"I'm sorry," she said.

He most definitely wasn't. "What for?"

"Walking out, coming back. Being flighty. I'm never flighty. I make a decision, I stick to it. I'm not needy, or clingy, I don't play games and I don't walk around with my head in the clouds. Grounded, that's me. I know my path, my goals, and I set out to achieve them."

"Maybe your path leads to me."

She softened beneath him then, and her bottom lip trembled slightly. And his heart was no longer simply in danger, it was fully compromised.

"How can it?" she asked, her voice a tremulous whisper. "This is not real."

"You feel very real to me."

"Simon—"

"Sophie." Then he kissed her, claimed her mouth as his own, wishing he could extend that declaration to the rest of her, but was thankful enough, for now, that she didn't turn him away. Thankful that, after only a moment, a breath, she kissed him back. Her fingers tunneled through his hair, her nails scraped his scalp as she pulled him closer, took the kiss deeper. As if perhaps she'd been hungering for him, missing him, as much as he had her. Two days. It felt like an eternity. Especially when he hadn't known he'd ever see her again.

He left her mouth, dropped kisses along her jaw, nuzzled her neck. She moaned softly, arching away from the door, into him, so she could tip her head back and allow him greater access. His body roared to life, the exhaustion and fatigue temporarily forgotten as desire and adrenaline punched renewed life into him. "I missed you."

"I missed you, too," she said on a sigh. "I didn't know what to think when Tolliver made his sudden move, and in the middle of the night."

He lifted his head so he could see her eyes. He framed her face, pushing his fingers into her soft tumble of curls. "I'm okay," he told her, answering her initial question. "Tolliver still doesn't know I'm here, as far as I can tell."

"Then why the sudden change? I thought maybe you'd made your move, and—"

"I did some scouting...." He didn't elaborate. It was bad enough he'd used her and her key tag. If she didn't know the particulars of where, how, or what had happened since then, she couldn't be liable. Well, as liable.

"I stayed home for two shifts, called in sick," she told him. "I wanted...to give you time. I had to have my tag replaced when I came back to work."

"Did it cause you trouble?"

She shook her head. "No. They issued me a new one."

He didn't even glance down at it. "I won't be wanting it, so don't worry."

"I couldn't risk it again, anyway. They let me off with a shake of the finger, but—"

He slid his thumbs across her lips. "I won't ask you to involve yourself further, Sophie."

"But what if I want—"

He stopped her with a kiss. "Just want this." He kissed her again, then again, until she was kissing him back. Only this time it wasn't simply the relief and thrill of being in each other's arms again. This time it flared quickly past that, as if they were both starving and had been presented with a buffet feast. Which was exactly how he felt about meeting Sophie. He hadn't known how hungry a man could be, how deprived he'd been, until presented with the most tantalizing smorgasbord he'd ever encountered. She swamped all of his senses, engaged him on every level. He'd never been so fully aware, so completely in tune, so insatiably greedy. *Want me*, he wanted to say. *Want me enough to stay, to try.*

He slid his hands down her body, pinning her to the door with his own as he pulled her legs up and urged them around him. "Hold on."

She wrapped her arms tightly around him, kissing the side of his neck and sending a whole new host of sensations rocketing through him as he spun her away from the door and staggered blindly toward the bed.

He found her mouth again, just as they hit the bed. He followed her down, then rolled to his side, pulling her with him, his lips never leaving her. She was undressing him, and he was, once again, fumbling with that damn maid's uniform. "You really have to stop wearing this thing," he murmured, as he tugged at the zipper while she popped open the buttons on his shirt.

"I know," she said, breathless. She got the last button of his shirt undone just as he tugged the zipper of her dress the last few inches. She shrugged out of her dress while he ripped his shirt off, his pants following.

He shoved them off the bed, then turned to find her struggling with her bra straps. "Allow me."

She smacked his hands away, then smiled when he looked affronted. "Oh no. You'll get sidetracked. And I'll let you. This time it's not going to just be about me."

"Well, I'm all for that, but—"

She slipped her arms from the straps, then pinned him to the bed by the shoulders when he reached for her again. "I'm not kidding. I don't know if or when I'll ever have this time with you again, and I'm not going to have any regrets."

He certainly didn't want to stop her from doing whatever the hell it was she wanted to do, but what she'd said, right before leaving him…they were too close now to chance it again. He had to know, had to make sure. "Before, when we were together, you said you didn't think you could handle taking things further—"

"That was before I spent two long days without you, wishing I hadn't been such an idiot."

He grinned. "I had a few wishes myself, but—"

She rolled fully on top of him. "I have no idea how I'll handle this, but I tried walking away, and that pretty much sucked. So, if it's going to suck either way, then I say we should at least have what we can have."

He rolled her to her back, pinned her wrists to the bed. Her chest was still heaving from the heavy breathing they'd already amped themselves up to. His breathing wasn't exactly steady either. "At the risk of destroying this not once, but twice, I have to ask you, who says this is all we can have?"

"Simon—"

He leaned down, bracing his weight on his elbows, smoothing a few errant curls from her face. He was surprised to feel the slightest tremor in his fingertips. He'd run dozens of jobs where steady fingers under extreme stress were the only thing between success and sometimes deadly failure. So it was disconcerting to say the least. But he knew that what happened here now, between them, was vital, paramount, even, to his future. "What do you want to have?" he asked quietly.

"Simon."

"I'm serious. If there were no boundaries, no obstacles, what would you want?"

She held his gaze for the longest time, and just when he thought she wouldn't answer, she whispered, "You."

He'd had no idea that the heart muscle could actually squeeze so painfully for reasons other than something like a heart attack. "What makes you think you can't have me?"

"Those boundaries and obstacles."

"Boundaries can be compromised, adapted to new needs. Obstacles can be overcome."

"You make it sound simple. It would be anything but. Simon, I…" She closed her eyes briefly, then opened them again and took a steadying breath. "Are you saying you want the same thing? Even if it's complicated? Really complicated?"

"I've never wanted anything so badly." And it was the God's honest truth. "It's what I was trying to tell you before. I couldn't leave you thinking it was just a lark. It was already more for me, or I wouldn't have said what I said."

"We don't really know each other."

"We know each other." He brushed a kiss across her lips. "I've never, not once in my life, been so fully engaged in another person. I don't know how long that's supposed to take, but with you it was instantaneous. And that fascination, that connection, has only strengthened the more time I spend with you, around you, listening to how your mind works, watching you." He kissed her again. "Smelling you, tasting you."

She moaned a little and arched into him when he took the kiss deeper, invaded her mouth, claimed her in the most basic way a man could claim a woman.

By the time he lifted his head, her body had grown heated and damp. His had, too. Her eyes were unfocused and dreamy looking, desire for him a naked, open thing.

"I hunger for you, Sophie. For everything about you. You may be right in that I don't know a lot about your life, and I have no idea what could become of us, but I do know you. You. And the need to find out the rest, the urge to explore this whatever it leads us to, is the strongest thing I've ever felt. When you walked out, it was like a part of me walked out with you. And I told myself how insane that was, but it's been two days, and it still feels exactly like that. It could be two years, and I don't think that would change. So it doesn't really matter how crazy this might be."

She slid her hand free and touched his face. Her fingers were shaky.

"Does that scare you?" he asked.

She nodded, but continued to stroke his face, his cheeks, his chin, his lips. Her fingertips might have been trembling, but her gaze never wavered from his.

"Good. Because it scares me, too," he said. "But it's also thrilling, and exciting, and fills me with this amazed sense of anticipation. This is too momentous a thing to walk away from just because I fear where it might take me, what it might cost me. That'll get me nothing."

"Chasing it could get you heartbreak," she said softly.

"Could. Life can be cruel, Soph. But, like you said, it can also be wondrous. Right now, the only heartbreak I feel is from not trying."

Her lips started to tremble again, and her eyes grew glassy.

"What did I say?" he asked, truly perplexed. "Don't cry."

"You're amazing, Simon Lassiter. And, I don't care what you say, you're rosy, and hopeful, and maybe even more of an optimist than I am. And I think your parents would be intensely proud of you right now."

"I want you to be proud. You. Sophie Maplethorpe. Of the soft curls, innocent freckles." He kissed one, then another. "Sharp mind, devilish wit." He kissed her forehead, the tip of her nose, the corner of her mouth. "And just a twisted enough view of how the world works to appeal to my rather eccentric views on the matter."

"Ditto," she said, then smiled through the sheen in her eyes. "Minus the freckles part."

"So, you'll have me, then, will you?"

She moved beneath him and this time he was the one who groaned. "I believe I will."

"Did I mention the wicked minx part?"

"Minx?" Laughter spurted from her. "Who uses that word?"

He moved between her legs and she gasped. "When it fits…"

He pushed into her, and she lifted her hips, wrapped her legs higher and took him fully. "Oh. My." She moved, gasped, then moved again. "It fits quite perfectly," she said, on a long, groaning sigh of satisfaction. "I thought, these past two days, I'd exaggerated how much." She moved beneath him. "If anything…I underestimated."

Simon knew exactly what she meant. He groaned and fought against the urge to pull out and plunge deeper, faster.

To take her with the furious need and heat that was a constant live thing inside him now. She was female in every single wonderful sense of the word. Delightfully soft beneath him, ample and strong, and so damn tight around him it was a miracle he could be still even a second.

"Have me, Simon," she whispered, then lifted her head and kissed him.

And he was well and truly lost to it, then. To her. Completely, utterly, and without a single reservation. It went against everything he'd ever been before. Every precaution he'd taken with his life, and more to the point, his heart. Gone as if they never existed. He'd seen what his parents had, and he'd never thought to be that lucky himself. Maybe that was why he'd never reached for it, never tried. They'd set the bar too high. Anything less would have been settling. Like Sophie, he knew what he wanted, and he went about getting it. But how did a person get that?

And yet, here it was. Right here. Finally. All he had to do was not screw it up. Find a way to keep it, keep her, and nourish and grow it, so it would be that powerful, amazing thing he'd witnessed firsthand.

And even that revelation didn't terrify him like it should.

The only thing that could terrify him now would be discovering her heart wasn't capable of making the same leap his was.

But, in that moment, his was pounding too hard and fast for him to pay any attention to what might come next. The only thing in his mind at this second was who was going to come right now.

_13_

A MILLION THOUGHTS RACED through her mind, but the sensations of Simon filling her, moving inside her, kissing her, swamped all of her senses and the jumble in her brain simply couldn't compete. So Sophie shoved the rest aside and gave herself over to the moment. And a more blissful, intense, deeply satisfying moment she'd never had.

He felt good on top of her, his weight, his body, covering hers. He was strong, and lean, and he was making love to her like she was the last woman on earth. It made her feel powerful, bold, intensely female. She lifted to meet each stroke, wanting more, faster, deeper. It was like she couldn't get enough, and she already knew that when it was over, she'd want him again. And again.

And the want, the need, wouldn't just be her body craving his. She wanted him around, in her life, in her bed, in her head, her heart, all of it.

She moved with him, and they quickly established a rhythm together, as he pushed deeper, making her cry out, wondering where this had been all her life. She felt such an intense satisfaction hearing him groan, then move faster still. She clutched at him, holding on as he started the climb, wanting nothing more than to drive him over the edge. Then he was lifting his face from the crook of her neck, weaving his fingers into her hair, turning her face to his. She lifted, expecting the kiss that would take them both there, but instead he just held her face until she opened her eyes, looking at him, while feeling him push harder, and tighten inside her.

"Sophie," he said, his voice ragged, his eyes so dark now.

"Yes," she said, not sure to what she was agreeing, but fairly certain she would to anything he asked of her in that moment.

"Don't run from this," he said, slowing just enough so that their gazes could remain locked. "After. Don't run."

It wasn't what she expected. To see that naked vulnerability in his eyes, hear it in his tone. Not begging, not demanding, just asking, in the most basic, elemental way a man could ask a woman. To stay. To try. "I won't," she whispered. "Promise."

The light that entered his eyes then was as fierce as it was triumphant, and her body, her mind, maybe even her soul, reacted to that moment in a way that scared and thrilled her... and had her moving with a whole new urgency, reaching for her own pinnacle, matching him, knowing she'd go over the edge when he did. It was wild, it was wonderful, and she didn't question it.

When he claimed her mouth as he let the moment take him, she tightened...and went with him.

It was stunning, like fireworks exploding, but all contained inside her body, as she was thrust into an oblivion of pleasure.

But it was the moments after, as their bodies slowed, and her heart didn't, that suddenly became the most powerful... and the most terrifying.

She'd promised him she wouldn't run. Wouldn't hide from this. Or shy away from the obstacles they'd encounter. At the moment, it was simply all too much to even contemplate. But the world wasn't going to stand still while she gathered her thoughts. The reality was, things were going to happen, events were scheduled that had to be considered, dealt with… and somehow, some way, she had to come to terms with all of that, and very quickly, if this was going to have even a prayer of moving forward past this moment.

"Simon—"

He rolled to his side, then pulled her into the shelter of his body and simply wrapped her up. "Not yet."

She'd never wanted shelter, needed to be held or coddled in any way. It usually made her a great partner, as the men of her previous acquaintance were more than happy to drift off into mindless sleep. Simon, on the other hand, didn't seem to be done communicating, his body to hers, just because the sex was over and the orgasms had been experienced. She thought it would feel suffocating, possessive. Instead, it felt…loving, and secure. An unspoken commitment.

She wasn't sure what her body was saying to him, but she'd never felt so at peace, and so…connected. Willingly and—shockingly—quite easily. This wasn't hard. In fact, it was wonderful, actually. So she gave in to the moment, savoring the newness of it, the profoundness of learning something about herself. And maybe something about the man Simon truly was, at the same time. She snuggled closer, slid her hand up to cover his heart, and let her eyes drift shut.

Later. Later she'd deal with what came next.

SOPHIE WAS ROUSED by the feeling of Simon kissing her temple, then the tip of her nose, the side of her chin. She stretched, feeling exactly like a cat must, after an afternoon spent napping in a sunbeam. Warmed throughout and more content than she could ever remember feeling. She fought to keep the storm of other thoughts at bay. She'd contend with all that, but she wasn't ready for the dream sequence part of her personal movie to end.

So she stretched, and rolled to her back, tugging him on

top of her, then slowly opened her eyes as she felt him ready for her again. "My," she teased, "what big—oh. Well." She grinned. "My, indeed."

He slid into her wordlessly, the look in his eyes softer, yet every bit as intense, as focused, as it had been last time, when their mating was furious and fast. This time it was anything but. It was lazy, languid, and quite wondrously perfect as he brought her slowly up, and tremblingly over, before he climbed there himself. It was only afterward, when he had, with a naturalness that made her eyes sting, pulled her close again, her back curved to his chest this time, his leg tucked over hers as he fell into a deep slumber, did she realize how well and truly he'd claimed her. And that her life would never, not ever, be the same again, now that Simon Lassiter had a piece of her heart.

"Not running," she breathed, letting her eyes drift shut, knowing sleep would be a long time coming. She had a lot of thinking to do. Only an idiot would walk away from this kind of man. She might have done some questionable things since meeting him, but this part wasn't in question. She was going to find a way to keep this. She tugged his arm more tightly around her. Keep him.

THIS TIME SHE WOKE FIRST. He still had the curtains drawn, so the room was cast in deep, dark shadows. She had no idea what time of day it was, and, for the moment, anyway, she didn't care. Instead, she carefully slipped from beneath the heavy weight of his arm and leg, and shifted around until she was on her side, facing him. Watching him. He looked less formidable while he was sleeping, but not exactly vulnerable. She studied his face, took her time looking at him, learning him. He was far, far, too pretty. In a rugged, intense kind of way. And he was hers. She looked up to the ceiling and smiled the smile of a woman who couldn't believe her good fortune.

Then she looked back at him, and the smile faded. Reality

began to make its slow, insidious return into her head, if not exactly her heart. And she had no choice now but to let it. In a few short hours, she would go back to work. She would, no doubt, be dealing with some kind of fallout from allowing Tolliver's hired pillars of beef to stand sentry. Delia would still believe that giving up her career to become a full-time Wingate Wife was a good idea, and that her husband-to-be would, at some point, stop being Cro-Magnon and treat her like his equal.

And the benefit gala would go on this weekend, and Simon would figure out some way to retrieve what he'd come for... or not. And then it would be time for him to return to his life abroad. Far away from her life here. She studied his face. How did a person conduct a relationship over such a long distance? Did he come to this country frequently? She supposed she could travel to his when her budget and time constraints allowed. Which would be basically never if she ever had hope of opening her own place. And what did his work entail, exactly? How much did he travel? Did he have an office? For that matter, where did he live?

The enormity of what she'd gotten her heart into really started to hit her. Because saying you would contend with the obstacles, that you'd find some way, that if you really wanted something, to figure it out, didn't exactly solve the problem, now did it? Easy to say, but where was the solution? She didn't see one. And she wasn't sure she was cut out for a partnership where she hardly ever actually saw her partner.

"You're killing me, you know," he murmured, his eyes still closed, his voice a gravelly mumble.

She started for a moment, wondering how long he'd been awake. "How am I doing that? I'm just lying here."

"Thinking," he said. "I can hear the wheels grinding from all the way over here. Speaking of which..."

He reached out and covered her hip with his hand, and the

next thing she knew, she was right back, flush up against him, tucked into the warm curve of his body.

He rested his cheek on the top of her head and nestled her closer. "Much better. Now quiet down in there."

She should have been annoyed, but she was smiling, which made the annoyed part much harder to sustain. Somehow, with him wrapped around her, so steady, so certain, it made it much easier to think there might be a solution. Maybe that was the trick. Staying close to him. Letting him be the one to keep reality at bay. Maybe he would figure it out and she wouldn't have to worry so much.

"Still grinding," he murmured, then pressed a warm kiss to her temple. He finally opened his eyes to stare deeply into hers. "Don't worry so much. Where there's a will…"

"I don't see the way," she whispered. "How can we—"

He cut her off with a short kiss, then heaved a deep sigh as he rolled her to her back and settled his weight half over her. His eyes were still dark with slumber and his hair was soft and tousled. His jaw was shadowed with the start of a morning beard, even though it had to be afternoon by now. He wasn't happy, but he wasn't annoyed, either. Just…steady.

"What?" she said, when he simply kept looking at her.

"How willing are you to think outside the box you've built for yourself here?"

"By box, do you mean my entire life?"

"Yes," he said succinctly.

"Wow. Well." She tried to mentally scramble through possible responses to that one, but he was too close, too serious, too…much. And she wanted all of it. To the point of it being a deep, aching, gaping chasm of want. "I'm willing," she said simply. Though she was convinced there couldn't be anything simple about this. Which figured, really. She'd finally found someone who could be The One, The Only, and of course, it was going to be impossible. She'd thought it was too good to be true that he'd want her as much as she wanted him, but it was true. So there had to be something else, right? The too good to be true part wasn't that he wanted her back, it was that they both wanted and couldn't have.

"So am I," he said, surprising her.

It hadn't occurred to her that maybe he'd be willing to make the adjustments.

"You look surprised," he said, pushing the hair from her face, his regard of her never wavering as sleep left his expression completely and the full-intensity Simon Lassiter returned.

She wished she could say that she'd feel better, more at ease, if he'd dial that part of him down, only it would be a lie. She liked everything about that intensity. Most especially, most very especially, when it was exclusively focused on her. "I wasn't thinking," she said. "I mean, I was thinking about how I could adjust things, make this work, find a way to see you after you go back, and—do you travel here a lot, then?"

"Sophie, I'm not interested in a commuter relationship with you."

Her eyes widened a bit, but she was rather proud of the steady, calm way she said, "Oh?"

"No," he responded.

"So…what, then? You're going to stay here? For me?" The very idea should have panicked her. A man she'd only just met, a man she wanted desperately to have a chance with, but still, a man she'd only known a few short days, was going to rearrange his entire life for her, a woman he'd just met. Yeah, terror would be the sane reaction to that possibility, on both fronts. So, where was the panic? The terror?

"I'm a grown-up, you know," he said, still toying with her hair, the slightest bit of twinkle surfacing in his otherwise still intent gaze. "I can put myself where I want to be. If it turns out I don't want to stay, or you don't want me to, I can always change paths again."

"Can it be as simple as all that? You just switching continents?"

"In some ways, yes."

She didn't say anything to that, and a few moments passed where he mercifully allowed it to sink in. "For me," she said. "Really."

"Really." He leaned in, kissed her chin. It made her heart tip, that perfect little gesture.

"Are you in the habit of making major life changes for someone you only just met?"

"Never. Not once." He smiled.

And she couldn't help it, she smiled back. "You're insane."

"I suppose it could look that way. I don't feel crazy, though. In fact, I feel bloody fantastic."

"That's just the sex talking."

"That feeling started before the sex," he said, "although I'm not averse to elevating fantastic to extraordinary from time to time. So, would you?"

"Would I what? Be averse to elevating...things? No, not at all." She moved her hips a little, and felt him respond.

"Hold that thought," he said, his voice a tad bit rougher. "What I meant was would you make such a leap? For a man you've only just met. Me, in this case."

It surprised her, the vulnerability she heard clearly in his request. He didn't even try to be casual or no-big-deal about it. Quite the opposite, really. And the idea that this big, strong, gun-toting, globe-trotting man could in any way be rendered less than one hundred percent sure of himself just sent another piece of her heart tipping his way.

"Had anyone asked me that three days ago, the response would have been a swift are-you-crazy followed by a hearty laugh." She smiled and reached up to smooth his bed head, and run her fingertips over the light stubble shadowing his jaw. "Now, however, I'd have to say that I'm certainly willing to consider it."

"A start, I suppose, right?"

She tugged a lock of his hair. "That's what all this is, isn't it? A start? And considering how we truly began, wouldn't it be surprising that any of this would have a normal evolutionary process? So how about you?"

"Did we just not discuss the possibility of my staying in your lovely country?"

"We did. But the pesky realist in me doesn't think you're going to just up and want to live in Chicago forever."

"People have been known to live in more than one place. I own land in New Zealand as well. My father's vineyard, in fact."

Her eyes widened. "Is it still operational?"

"Oh, yes. Once he figured out that I was unlikely to follow in his immediate footsteps, he looked at his own staff, and worked from there."

"Is he still…?"

"Alive?" Simon shook his head. "He poured himself into work after my mum died, but I don't think he was ever the same. He had his share of health issues, and without my mother there to nag him, he didn't take as good care of himself as he might have otherwise. I offered to come back, help him, but he knew I was finding my own way and turned me down, whenever I'd make the offer. I did go back, several times, anyway. After his first heart attack, then again, later when his new manager in chief contacted me to let me know he was declining."

"And?"

"And, he's a smart man, my father, at least when it comes to safeguarding the business he spent a lifetime building. He chose well in who he trained to manage it, and in setting things up legally so that it stayed in the family. It was his legacy to me and my future offspring, but he wanted to ensure it was run well in his—and my—absence. I think…" He trailed off, until Sophie brushed her fingers over his forehead, pushed at his hair.

"You think, what? That he wasn't as interested in living without your mom?"

He nodded. "I was there, when he went. And he was almost relieved. He fully believed they would be reunited."

"I think that's a perfectly wonderful thing to leave this world believing."

He smiled and kissed her nose. "It took me a bit longer to get past being mad at him for not trying harder to take care of himself. But, in the end, I did have to accept, as he'd told me often enough, that he was captain of his own destiny. As I was of mine. He wanted to leave me what he'd built, but that was because it was important to him. He told me, both personally and in his will, that what happened to the vineyard after his passing is up to me, and I'll have his blessing regardless."

"Have you thought about it? What you want to do about it?"

"Right now, I have the luxury of not worrying. It's only been a few years since he's been gone and it's in very good hands. At some point, when Mac wants to retire, depending on who he's groomed, and how the place is faring, and what is going on in my life, I'll have some important decisions to make. But, fortunately for me, not today. Or tomorrow."

"You're a very lucky man. To have the love and support you've had. Particularly given your path hasn't exactly been what most people would call typical. How did you get started doing what you're doing? Were you—or are you—some kind of private detective?"

"Actually, my degree is in archaeology."

"Really."

He smiled dryly. "Seriously."

She swatted him; he laughed. "So, how did you go from being Indiana Jones to being a retrieval specialist?"

"Well, archaeologists are retrieval specialists, of a sort. I was working for a university outside London after getting my degree, hoping to get on to one of the dig teams, help raise funding, whatever I could, and my professor mentioned a problem he was having, trying to track down a personal item he'd lost on his last dig site. In Egypt."

"So...you found it?"

Simon shrugged. "I admit, I was trying to impress the guy. I really wanted to be on the team."

"Did he pick you?"

"Well, he certainly would have, he was very impressed with my initiative, but in mentioning it to a colleague of his, there was talk of a family heirloom that had been put up for auction, and a question if perhaps I could look into it."

"And you did."

He nodded.

"And you found it."

"It took some doing. I wasn't aware, when I agreed, that it had been put up for auction in the eighteen hundreds."

Sophie's eyes rounded. "And you actually located it?"

"Well, in this case, it had been rightfully purchased, several times over, but eventually, yes. So—"

"You put the parties together and they came up with an equitable solution. Like the marbles."

"Something like that, yes. And, I suppose, as you say, the rest is history."

"What about your passion for archaeology? Do you miss it?"

"I wonder about it, at times, where it might have taken me, but this sort of odd niche I've carved for myself is fulfilling in much the same way. I'm not uncovering details of the ancient past, or finding new information about the history of our world, but I am delving into a far more intimate, personal history of whoever it is I take on as a client. It's still digging, still uncovering clues, just of a slightly different nature." He kissed her. "I know it doesn't sound like the most stable way to earn a living, but I've been at it for some time now, and my list of contacts keeps growing. Plus, I've only had myself to take care of, so I've had plenty of time to invest wisely. My father taught me well." He smiled. "Some things, anyway."

"I think what's most important is that you found something that fulfills you and that you really enjoy."

"I have, and I do. What about you? Why hotel management?"

"I grew up pretty much in the kitchen of my grandmother Winnifred's restaurant. Studying after school, working when I was old enough. She had such a passion for people, and for food. Her place was a home away from home for me and a lot of regulars. It's incredibly hard work, but I thought it would be a great way to spend a life."

"But?"

She made a face. "I can't so much as boil water. Something you should know."

"Handy you work in a hotel with round-the-clock kitchen service."

She grinned. "I know. Good planning, right? I knew I wanted to do something in the service industry, but that it wouldn't be running my grandmother's restaurant. My aunt took it over when her health wouldn't allow her to run it full-time, and eventually her husband took it on."

"Is it still here? In Chicago?"

She shook her head. "No, he's from Philadelphia originally, and his son opened a place there, and when my aunt passed on, he moved east to run the place with him. We talk when we can, keep in touch, but I don't see them very often."

"Any other family here?"

She shook her head. "I'm it."

"So, how did you decide on hotels?"

"Well, I don't really aspire to run a huge hotel, but if I want to eventually open up my own inn, then this is where the money is at, and the hands-on education earned along the way will be invaluable, no matter what scale the place is I eventually open."

"You want to open your own place, then?"

She smiled, and her expression went slightly shy, but excited at the same time. "That's the plan. Long-term plan, but the plan. I'm not sure where. I don't know that I want to stay in the city. I have in mind something more intimate, more of a getaway-type place. But, who knows? Like you said, it's not something I have to worry about today. Or tomorrow. I have a ladder to climb, first. And a nest egg to grow."

"I have every faith."

"You know, that means a lot. And I'm lucky in that my friends, the ones I've made here at the hotel, who are close enough to know my dreams, are all rooting for me. But sometimes I miss the family aspect of it, that lifelong foundation. I'm not complaining, mind you. Just saying."

"I know what you mean. I feel the same about home. About my family."

"Do you spend much time there? New Zealand, I mean."

"Not as much as I used to, or as much as I'd want. Work has kept me in London more and more. It's central to a larger community demanding my services. But, I've been thinking...I imagine there are folks here in your lovely country who might find my services attractive, and Chicago is rather central, as well. And you all have far less heritage to be researched. Could make my job loads easier."

"You'd do that?"

"I'd certainly give it a try."

"I'd guess you'd need to travel a lot. Overseas. Keep up with those clients."

"I already told you that I'm not in the market for a long-distance relationship, but, from time to time, if one of my longtime clients makes a request, I'd have to at least consider it. You could certainly accompany me, if it was possible."

"That would depend on my position at the time. As soon as I move to day management, I'll probably be living here, more often than not. They even work out deals for managers to do just that."

He grinned. "I have a small flat in London, and one in Sydney, but I spend most of my life in hotels. So that wouldn't be a big adjustment for me."

"Just as long as you don't go cavorting about in other people's hotels, picking up accomplice maids as you go."

He kissed her again, then again. "You're the only accomplice maid for me."

She grinned, then laughed as he nuzzled her neck. "Good. And don't you forget, it's not every accomplice maid who can do lousy Russian-Asian-Spanish accents."

"I know, right? Can I pick them, or what?" He lifted his head, and stared down into her face, and he looked so...happy. Joyful. It made her heart swell right up until she thought it might burst.

"Yes," she said, more sincerely than she'd intended. "And can I say, I'm so very glad you did?"

"You can," he said, then began kissing her along her jaw, before taking her mouth and kissing her deeply and quite intently. All teasing was gone, but when he lifted his head, the openness was still there.

"Remember when I said before, that I decide on a path, a goal, and I work toward it. I haven't any clue what choices I'll be willing to make, or what I can and can't live with. But I suppose that's true of any new step a person takes, whether it's personal or professional. I have never let the fear of failure keep me from going for anything I wanted. I guess that's why I came back to your room. It wasn't like me to chicken out. I'd have never made it two days in this industry if that was the case."

He framed her face with his hands, and kept his gaze on hers. He didn't interrupt, and he didn't hurry her. But his steady regard, his willingness to allow her to say whatever it was she had to say, however she had to say it, gave her enormous faith in how they'd progress from this point on.

She smiled. "So…this is me. Not being a chicken." She lifted her head enough to kiss him. "How do you feel about being my new goal?"

"Pretty bloody fantastic."

"Hmm," she said. "Only bloody fantastic? Not extraordinary?" She rolled him to his back and straddled his hips, pinning his hands over his head. "I see I have my work cut out for me."

He tilted his head back and closed his eyes. "Have I mentioned how much respect I have for your dedicated work ethic?" Then he groaned, long and deep, and with great satisfaction as she went about making certain she'd earned that respect.

14

"I'm not really cut out for this," Sophie called through the closed bathroom door. "Literally," Simon heard her mutter.

"Your body was made to wear dresses like that. Men will drool, women will wish they could fill it out like you do. Come out so I can see it."

"Oh, I fill it out, all right. My body might have been made for dresses like this, but clearly dresses like this were not made for my body. If I so much as take a deep breath, we're talking wardrobe malfunction of humiliating proportions."

"Come out, or I'm coming in."

The door opened. His heart stopped. "Wow."

"From the way you just went pale, I'm guessing that's not a good 'wow,' huh?"

"Maybe the femme fatale thing wasn't such a good strategy."

Rather than look hurt or insulted, she looked triumphant. And more than a little relieved. That was why his heart was no longer his to command. With Sophie, it was about getting the job done, whatever the job might be. Vanity and ego rarely entered into it, which made her confidence in herself a million times sexier.

"I told you," she said, openly smug. "Now, help me get

out of this body-length tourniquet." She turned around and presented him with the rear view. "The zipper is stuck halfway up."

He had no idea where the zipper was, not that he could tell her. His throat had turned to dust. The rest of him, however, had turned into a raging inferno of testosterone. He'd gotten this dress mostly to fulfill their plan of attack, but also as a test for himself. He didn't like the possessive, jealous side she brought out in him, and had hoped that with their freshly forged commitment to trying to be together as a team—though she'd already pushed the teamwork aspect way further than he'd been prepared to let her—he might settle back into the rational, sensible male he'd always been up to the day he'd met her.

Apparently that man had not made a return engagement. Not where parading her around in something that made her look like sex on a stick was concerned. And it had absolutely nothing to do with trust. And everything to do with men ogling her, fantasizing about her, picturing her as he very well knew they'd be picturing her, because he most certainly was. It made him want to behave quite...primitively. "Wow," he said again, not wanting to damn himself in any other way. It was his problem, not hers.

There was a pause, then she said, "Okay, that didn't sound like such a bad wow."

"Trust me," he choked out. "All good."

"Very funny." She looked over her shoulder, but her indulgent smile immediately turned to one of wariness and she turned fully around. "Okay, now you're looking like you want to drag me into the nearest cave by my hair."

"Amazingly accurate description," he said, a hunger welling up in him that dwarfed all that had come before it.

"Simon, you picked the thing out, so you can hardly—"

"My goal, at the time, was to put you in something that

would attract attention on a large scale, and give you entrée to Tolliver and his significant other's inner circle at the gala."

"And?"

"And…" He trailed off, looking again at how the emerald-green dress with the plunging neckline and the barely there back hugged her siren curves in a way that would have made Marilyn Monroe envious. "*Wow* might not be a terribly astute description, but it really sort of sums it up."

"Are you going to help me take it off or not?"

He stepped closer. "Oh, I want to rip it from your body. With my teeth." He stepped closer still. "Then take you up against the nearest wall." Another step. "In the chair by the window. Across the foot of the bed." Another step, which backed her up against the sink. "And anywhere else I can have you."

He saw her visibly gulp. "Wow," she breathed.

"Exactly. I'm feeling like I've suddenly been given thirty years' worth of Christmas presents to unwrap all in the form of a single, perfect package."

"The things you say…" Her eyes were wide, and fixed on his.

"The things you make me feel," he responded.

"I don't know whether to be flattered that I can affect you like that, or worried that you really are going to drag me off by my hair." Her lips quirked a little. "Mostly because I might find out I like it when you get all caveman on me." Her lips bowed into a soft curve. "How politically incorrect of me."

And that was the Sophie he was falling in love with; the femme fatale in the green dress who made jokes at her own expense, and still had no idea of her true power. He was so well and truly gone. He'd have asked her to marry him on the spot if he thought she'd take him seriously.

He framed her face with his palms. "How is it that no man has dragged you off as yet?"

"Gosh," she said dryly, "hard to imagine."

"Truly," he said, quite sincere, "it is. The idea of taking you out in that is nerve-racking."

She covered his hands with her own and pulled them, joined, between them. "Why? Don't you think I can handle myself? I mean, I might not be the most natural—"

"You're a born natural. Thank God you're the only one who doesn't know it or you could rule the world by sundown."

"You are the best ego boost a girl could ever have, you know that?"

"I say what I mean. I think you can more than handle yourself. And I think it's that very uncertainty you seem to have about your impact, though God knows why with the mirrors right behind you telling the story, that will make tonight a smashing success."

"Then why are you worried?"

He pulled her into his arms, trapping her hands between them. "Because if, at any point, you do discover just what amazing powers you wield, I'm afraid you'll ditch me for the nearest bloke with a local address and a winning smile."

"You think me as shallow as all that, do you?" She was smiling when she said it, clearly not believing him even remotely.

"I no longer know what to think," he said, then dipped his chin, resting his forehead on hers. "This is uncharted territory for me, this possessive streak, this…this…jealousy. I'm not fond of it, I must admit."

"I can't believe you." She tipped his face back up to hers. "Talk about a man who wields weapons. Have you looked in the mirror lately, sir? What if we go out and you're swamped by women who actually wear clothes like this as a regular course of action? What prayer do I have?"

"You're being ridiculous. I'm completely besotted."

"Ditto." She gave him a smacking kiss. "So, shut up already."

He jerked her more tightly against him, and kissed her

back so fiercely it was a miracle they both didn't burst into a spontaneous inferno.

When he broke the kiss, her eyes were unfocused and her mouth…dear heavens, her mouth. His body both trembled and simultaneously made him feel like he could leap buildings in a single bound. "The need I have for you…this can't be sane."

"Simon," she said, rather shakily, "has it ever occurred to you that this…thing, this…whatever the hell connection it is we share, is a force to contend with because we share it? If we can trust in it—"

"That's just it. It's hard to trust in something I can't even explain. I feel like it would be more rational for it to vanish as swiftly as it arrived. Rather like you're Cinderella at the ball, and I'm the poor bloke who'll be left with nothing more than the glass slipper and the harsh reality that it was all a fantasy after it's over."

"Simon—"

"Sophie," he said, on a sigh. "I'm being quite ridiculous, you don't have to tell me that. I just need to—"

"Believe in me," she said, then smoothed her hand over his cheek and brushed the hair at his temple. "Believe in us. Believe that we'll do our best, and stick by each other. Take on the world, and see what happens. Beyond that, there are no guarantees, right? What happens, will happen."

He smiled then, and his heart settled a bit. "Think you're so smart, do you?"

"I have a lot more faith in my smarts than I do in this dress," she said, "but I'll tell you, the way you look at me in this dress makes me feel like I can conquer the world." She slipped her hands in his and squeezed. "And that's what really matters, right?"

"You're amazing."

"I'm terrified," she said. "But not of us. Us excites me, and exhilarates me. My only hope of having any success at that gala tonight is with you at my side."

"Ditto, Miss Maplethorpe."

"Well, I wouldn't get too attached to that idea. We both know my track record in hotel espionage. So far, it's two-to-zip against. You sure you want to even try this? Maybe you should go alone. Maybe—"

"What happened to conquering the world?"

"I'd rather conquer a world where there are less potential felonies involved. And no heels. Work my way up."

He grinned. "You'll be fine. I might have a heart attack every time I look at you in that dress, and there could be fireworks if Tolliver so much as winks, but—"

"Isn't that the whole point? To get his attention?"

"Not that kind of attention. You're supposed to work your way into his inner circle, then hover until his—"

"Business associate?" she filled in dryly.

"Whoever she is. When she takes a break for the ladies room, you need to be with her. It's our only chance."

"And where will you be, again? If you can't let Tolliver see you, then how—."

"Just as I explained. I'll be there. It's going to be very, very crowded. It won't be difficult for me to stay close by without being seen."

"You're wearing that, right?" She nodded to the tux that was hanging on the back of the door.

He nodded.

"You'll be seen. Women will flock, find excuses to be near you. You'll draw attention. Trust me."

"The room will be filled with men in tuxedos."

"Trust me," she repeated.

He squeezed her hands now. "You'll have to trust me. I might not have a clue how to handle you in that dress, but with this, I do know what I'm doing."

"I believe that. Just as I believe that, when the night is over, you'll know exactly how to handle me in this dress. Or out of it."

"You know how to provide proper motivation, I'll give you that."

"I might totally stink at the actual espionage part, but I talk a good game."

"Well, talking is all that is expected of you this evening."

"Speaking of which, when I make my trip to the ladies' room, then what? I mean, I know you said you'd be around—"

"Just stall long enough to make sure I have enough time to get from wherever I am to that area. I'll take care of it from there."

For the first time, she frowned. "You'll take care of it how, exactly?

He smiled, hoping it was reassuring. "How a professional takes care of things."

"Simon—"

"Sophie," he admonished. "We went over this. I am forever grateful to have you on my side in this, but I really don't want you involved any more than you have to be."

"Need-to-know basis," she said, somewhat dryly.

"More or less, yes."

She didn't argue the point. They'd already done that, and while she'd made her case for helping him out, he'd stood his ground on not involving her beyond helping to set up the situation.

"What about after?" she asked.

"I'll need to leave the country." At her alarmed look, he quickly kissed her and added, "Just to return the emerald to Guinn. Then I'll need to settle things in London while I'm there. And…make certain I'm not going to have Tolliver trolling after me, and, therefore, you."

"Is that a strong possibility?"

"I'm sure we'll have a talk."

"A talk."

"Trust me, okay?"

"I'm trying. But you may have to reassure me. A lot. Not about being gone—I completely understand about that. I'd go with you if I could take the time away from here. But about Tolliver, and you being safe. I'll want to know you're safe."

"Done." He turned her around and tugged her zipper the rest of the way up. "Now, how about we go get Guinn's birthright back?"

"I never asked—how did you figure it out? That it rightfully belonged to Guinn? Did you find proof?"

"No. I can't prove it's his. And I can't prove Tolliver faked those documents. Not without access to them, which, of course, he won't give me at this point. Had I known at the time I did have my hands on them, I would have called in some favors and done every test available. I only did some cursory checking on them because I fully believed Tolliver's claims, and all the other bull he'd been feeding me."

"What changed?"

"Getting to know Guinn. And knowing what was in my gut. After first meeting him, despite Tolliver's claims I felt sorry for him even then, but I had what I thought was ironclad proof. And a belief that Tolliver was a good man, with good intentions. I soon learned otherwise, partly on my own, and partly through Guinn."

"But it was too late?"

"Far too late. I confronted Tolliver about it, tried to get him to do the right thing, and was quickly shown the door and threatened with the ruination of my career if I pursued it."

"But you did."

"I did. And, so far, respect for my skills hasn't diminished in the circles I move in, but that is partly due to the fact that when I got it wrong, which I did, I immediately went to work to make it right."

"What if we can't get it back?"

Simon shook his head. "I wronged a man who didn't

deserve it, and this will be the last chance he will have, in his lifetime, to right another wrong done to ancestors of his who were also swayed by the powerful, persuasive rhetoric of past members of Tolliver's family. I have to get it back."

She smiled, and slipped the bag containing his tux off the back of the door. "Then you might want to go put this on. The show is about to start."

"What did I do to deserve you again?"

She bussed him on his lips. "Um, tied me to a hotel chair until I could discover for myself that you are an amazing, fantastic man whom I'm happy to help steal priceless gemstones for?"

He grinned. "Oh yeah. That."

"Now, hurry up. I can only pretend I can breathe in this for so long."

15

SOPHIE TRIED TO PRETEND she was Julia Roberts, making her grand entrance at the end of *Pretty Woman*. There were some very gratifying, confidence-boosting double takes, and a few conversations that went silent as she made her way through the crowded room, but, mostly, Sophie didn't think Julia had anything to worry about. If Sophie could find Tolliver before she disgraced herself by falling off the impossibly high heels she was wearing and into a platter of passing crab canapés, she'd consider it a job well done.

Having seen Tolliver at his less-than-commanding best, it was Sophie who did a double take when she finally spotted him, standing near one of the cases displaying part of his collection. In this instance, the tux definitely made the man. He stood out, even in a sea of custom-cut tuxedos. His gleaming silver hair was a far cry from the damp, stringy mess she'd seen, postshower. Instead, it was quite the elegantly styled, leonine mane, shown off to great distinction by the black-on-black perfectly tailored tux, with a single-button jacket, placard-front shirt and expertly knotted silk bow tie. His laughter was rich and melodic, and carried effortlessly over the conversational noise of the crowded room, naturally drawing people closer.

Sophie was part of that wave, trying to look both conspicuous and inconspicuous at the same time and likely not pulling off either. As she approached, she could hear snippets of his conversation and marveled at how completely different he was here, in this setting, than he had been in the privacy of his suite. Granted, there he'd been quite upset, unlike here where he was making contacts and trying to impress people. But she'd have never thought the man she'd inadvertently met just out of the shower could ever transform himself into this charming, elegant leading man. Sean Connery could take lessons.

She could only hope her change in appearance was equally dramatic, so there would be no chance he'd recognize her as the maid who'd trespassed into his room. And then the time to worry was over, as the ebb and flow of the crowd flowed more than it ebbed, literally pushing her directly into his immediate circle of sycophantic followers and hangers-on.

Conversation stuttered to a halt as she barely righted herself with the help of someone's hand on her elbow, then turned to thank them with what she hoped was a gracious, apologetic smile. "I'm so sorry."

It was Tolliver's hand on her elbow. She hoped she hadn't gone completely pale. Her smile was frozen as she tried to swallow past the sudden tightness in her throat.

"My, my," he murmured. "I'm not remotely sorry. Good evening, Miss...?"

How was it that the voice that had been so chilling, so soulless, so...dead, was now so warm and lively? She carefully withdrew her elbow from his light grasp, apologized to the gentleman next to Tolliver, whose foot she'd just missed puncturing with her heel, then turned to face him again with what she hoped was a natural-looking smile. "Maplethorpe. Sophie Maplethorpe."

She extended her hand, which he quite gallantly lifted as he bowed over it. Fortunately he'd stopped short of kissing the back, as she didn't really want to find out exactly where Simon was quite yet. Nor did she need to add nausea to the list of things already making her supremely uncomfortable. "A pleasure to meet you, Mr. Tolliver. Quite the collection you've put on display here. I'm sure my fellow Chicagoans agree that we're fortunate to be the recipients of such generosity."

My, my, indeed. Wasn't she suddenly just the chatty little socialite? Maybe Julia Roberts should watch out after all. She swallowed again and tried to maintain direct, easy eye contact.

"Why, thank you. I'm so pleased to hear you think so. And, call me Langston." He turned to the stunning brunette standing next to him, who was presently looking daggers at Sophie, but who smiled quite impressively when cued. "Please allow me to introduce my guest this evening, Marcelina Brand."

Look at her face, look at her face, Sophie schooled herself. Which shouldn't have been all that difficult. Millions had before her, as Marcelina's exquisite visage had graced numerous billboards and magazine covers. But it was almost an impossible assignment when she was wearing a huge, honking emerald necklace around her neck. Sophie tried to remember her as the giggling bimbo from the shower, but staring at Marcelina now, it was hard to believe she'd ever cracked a real smile, much less a laugh.

Realizing she was gawking, though she assumed Marcelina was quite used to it, probably expected it, given the rather bored expression on her face, Sophie quickly extended her hand for a brief, feminine hand-clasp before giving up the battle entirely and simply staring at the stunning array of stones covering the full stretch of the supermodel's neck and collarbones. "That is an amazing, amazing piece you're wearing. Did you have it specially designed?"

"Thank you," Marcelina said, managing to sound all breathless sex-kitteny, even as her green-eyed gaze said careful-or-

I'll-cut-you-bitch. "For some reason, Langston thought I was the one to showcase them."

Sophie had heard the word *cooed* used to describe a tone of speech, but, until now, she'd never heard it in action.

Marcelina slid her arm possessively through Tolliver's and Sophie wanted to reassure the supermodel that she was quite safe from any attempt at poaching her date. As if Sophie had a prayer. In fact, that Marcelina felt the need to make a public show of claiming him at all was rather unbelievable. Like any sane man would switch partners while she was on his arm.

"I don't see how he could have chosen anyone better," Sophie said, part of her marveling at how well she was maintaining the flow of conversation in such a surreal situation, even as her mouth continued to move and words continued to come out. "I can't imagine how it feels to wear something like that."

"Priceless," Tolliver interjected. "The feeling of wearing the Shay emerald is as priceless as the piece itself." He covered Marcelina's hand with his own, but his gaze was focused purely on Sophie. "I believe it would turn any woman into a piece of art."

Marcelina frowned slightly, as if she wasn't quite sure if she'd been properly complimented—Sophie doubted she'd ever even consider she'd been insulted—but then must have realized she was wrinkling her perfect skin and immediately smoothed her expression to one of bored tolerance.

"You look quite familiar, my dear," Tolliver was saying. "Where would our paths have crossed?"

Sophie's heart came to a full stop, then raced ahead like a rabbit. "I beg your pardon?" she managed, as if she hadn't properly heard the question, still so taken with the radiance of the necklace. She smiled brightly. Well, mostly, she tried not to throw up on the man's shiny black leather shoes.

"I don't recall meeting her," Marcelina was saying.

"Darling, I meet people every day," he said dismissively, still gazing at Sophie.

"We haven't met," Sophie assured her quickly, before Marcelina could stab her with a hairpin, which, if the look in her blazing green eyes was any indication, she was a heartbeat away from doing. "I work for the Wingate. In fact, I helped with the new security detail you requested. But we didn't meet."

"Perhaps that's it then," he said, smiling quite congenially. "I'm quite certain I'd have remembered specifics had we met face-to-face." He took her hand again, and bowed. "A woman who could put a work of art to shame with just her smile."

My, my, Sophie thought, wanting desperately to press a hand to her stomach. He really was quite the smooth one.

"So, you're here in some kind of professional capacity, then?" Marcelina asked, her interest clearly feigned, as if she was being hard-pressed to be nice to the help, but managing all the same for the sake of appearances.

Sophie assumed she'd had tons of practice with that. "Why no," she said, slipping her hand from Tolliver's once again and turning her brightest smile toward the model. "Why do you ask?"

Marcelina lifted a slender shoulder, as if she could hardly be bothered to respond, now bored with the conversation. "I assumed the Wingate must be catering the affair or some such. After all, the guest list is quite…" She ran her gaze over Sophie, from her self-styled hair to her store-bought heels. "…exclusive."

"Actually, she's with me," came a feminine voice from behind Sophie. "Us, I should say."

Delia. Sophie turned with the first honest smile she'd had all night. "And Adam," she finished out loud, surprised to see him, though she couldn't have said why. Mrs. Wingate was nothing if not clever in her campaign to earn as much media attention as possible. If she couldn't get the Art Institute to change the date, she'd simply make sure the Wingate family was represented at the gala and garnered some of the spotlight away from the event, during the event.

Still it was a surprise that Arlene had employed her about-to-be-married son and soon-to-be daughter-in-law in the battle, considering the packed calendar of duties that Sophie knew firsthand from her friend was dominating literally every second of her waking hours until the wedding began. In fact, Sophie wouldn't have been the least bit surprised if Arlene had ordered instructional subliminal recordings to be played while Delia slept.

"What a pleasure to meet the happy couple," Tolliver said, his charm not ebbing for so much as a millisecond. "I've heard so much about you both. I trust everything is moving along smoothly with the upcoming nuptials?"

Delia stepped forward and gave Marcelina a direct snub by taking Tolliver's hand and favoring him with a smile, while appearing not to notice that he was there with a guest. Much less a guest of such international acclaim. Sophie wanted to applaud, but she felt it would be in poor taste.

"Why yes, thank you, Mr. Tolliver. It's been a true fairy tale, from beginning to end."

Sophie's urge to applaud continued, but now it was for the complete transformation of her best friend. She'd sounded so…sincere. And she truly looked like Cinderella at the ball. Her blond hair in a perfectly coiffed chignon, elegant, shimmering blue gown, diamonds and sapphires on her ears and around her neck. Who was this perfect princess? Certainly not the same woman Sophie had consumed copious amounts of almond rocca and Chunky Monkey ice cream with after yet another bad date or failed relationship.

"Not that there will be an end," Adam so perfectly interjected, smiling his handsome Prince Charming smile as he reached out to pump Tolliver's hand.

"Well, and who wouldn't live happily-ever-after with such

a stunning bride on his arm," Tolliver said. "I wish you both the best."

"Thank you," Delia said. "So, Mr. Tolliver, tell us about your collection. Very impressive. And it's all from your personal ancestry?"

"You must call me Langston," he said, before launching into a detailed description of the various pieces.

Sophie took a much needed moment to regroup and step out of the immediate spotlight, listening with half an ear, but privately scanning the crowd to see if she could spot Simon.

Then Marcelina, apparently upset with not being the center of attention for more than thirty seconds, took possession of Tolliver once more by leaning closer and saying, quite petulantly, "I'm still waiting on my drink, darling."

"Come with me," Adam said, jumping in like a man rescued, then winked at Tolliver. "I'm sure you won't mind if I steal your stunning date away for a moment." He laughed then, and added, "I've only another night as a free man, so it will be the last time I can be seen with such a lovely woman on my arm who isn't my wife without raising a scandal."

Everyone smiled and laughed, because Adam's golden boy good looks and beaming confidence—not to mention his bank account—demanded it, but Sophie could only look at Delia, who did a remarkable job of hiding her disappointment in once again being ignored by her fiancé and left standing without so much as a backward glance, much less a drink order, as he took off with Marcelina. Sophie imagined Delia hadn't missed the fact that Adam took the time to work the room with the supermodel on his arm, as he traveled a very circuitous route to one of the several bars that had been set up for the night's event.

Unfortunately, Sophie was so caught up watching her friend attempting to mask her disappointment, that she missed spying on Tolliver to see if he'd sent any kind of signal to anyone to follow Marcelina. Maybe he felt she was in safe hands, given

Adam's superstar status in the room. The entire event, for that matter, was heavily, and quite visibly secure, making her wonder how Simon planned on removing the piece from the premises even if he could get it away from the model.

"Yes, there has been a lot of attention. *People* magazine will be doing a spread," Delia was saying. "We just confirmed today."

Sophie turned her attention back to the conversation at hand, wishing she could follow Marcelina and Adam—or, more to the point, the necklace. But with Tolliver's date and Delia's date abandoning them, it rather forced them to remain and make small talk. Sophie could have likely come up with some reason to excuse herself before she lost sight of the couple, and might have, if it weren't for the death grip Delia now had on her arm.

"You must be so thrilled," exclaimed a female member of the small throng enveloping Tolliver, Delia and Sophie in a circle of attention.

"Yes, it's all very exciting," Delia responded, sounding slightly less authentically enthused than she had moments before.

"You know," Sophie said brightly, sliding her arm through Delia's, "with the whirlwind of events, we've barely been able to get two seconds alone." She beamed at the group, then looked at Tolliver. "Would it be horribly rude if I stole her away for a few moments?"

"No, no," Tolliver assured her, already turning his attentions to another twentysomething ingénue who had joined their circle. "It was a pleasure making both of your acquaintances," he said with a brief smile, then was fully engaged in his new conversation, bowing over another slender hand, before they'd even broken the sycophant circle.

"Thank God," Sophie breathed, as they cleared the group. She immediately scanned the room, but had completely lost sight of Adam and Marcelina. A quick look back at the cluster around Tolliver didn't show any obvious muscle lurking about. She'd been too stunned by the change in his appearance and demeanor to make note of that earlier when she'd first approached the group.

Then Delia was all but dragging her off to the side of the room they were in, ducking them both around behind another display. "I was so surprised to see you here. Why didn't you tell me? And where in the world did you get that dress? You look really amazing. I can't believe it's you."

"Thanks," Sophie said dryly, "I think."

"I didn't mean it like that. I just had no idea you'd be here. Why are you here? And who are you with? I can't believe you didn't tell me."

"Ditto. Although you making the guest list is far less surprising than me making it. Still, I'm amazed Arlene let you two out of her evil clutches for so much as five minutes. I figured she'd have you both in shackles until you were standing in front of clergy."

"We weren't supposed to be here, but she decided it was an 'advantageous opportunity' to talk about the *People* magazine spread and—"

"Steal the spotlight away from the very worthy cause the benefit is promoting and hog the media wherever possible?" Sophie finished brightly, then immediately recanted when her friend's expression wobbled. "I'm sorry. But, come on, it's not like we haven't both bashed Arlene before when we've had the chance. You and I both know she's a barracuda, but I shouldn't have been so thoughtless with everything you must be going through. It's almost over," she said, rubbing her arm. "Day after tomorrow."

"I know," Delia said, but she clearly wasn't really paying attention to Sophie.

"What? What is it, Dee? What's wrong?"

Dee pulled her farther into the shadows, leaving Sophie to pray that Simon had somehow seen Marcelina and Adam's defection and was, right this very second, hot on their trail. "What's going on?"

"Nothing. Everything." Delia's eyes grew suspiciously glassy. "I don't know."

"Is there a problem? Did something happen?"

"Remember how I told you earlier this week that I'd de-cided to just fully commit myself to becoming a full-fledged Wingate wife, that my goal was to be the partner Adam truly needed and desired?"

Uh-oh. "Yes, of course I remember. Why, is Arlene giving you a hard time again? Did his sisters say something? Because, if you truly love him and want to support him, you're going to have to find a way to develop a thick skin with them. In fact, I think it's high time you considered standing up a little for yourself where they are concerned. Otherwise I'm afraid they're going to make your life miserable forever."

Dee's eyes went from glassy to teary. She dabbed at the corners as first one tear escaped, then another. "Oh God," she said, "I can't cry. Not here, not now. If anyone sees me crying, it will be a spectacle. Arlene hates spectacles, and so does Adam. Unless, of course, they're the ones creating the spectacle, then all bets are off."

It was the first time in a while that Sophie had heard that particular tone in her friend's voice. "Come on, we'll find the ladies' room, do a quick repair."

"There is no quick repair that will fix this," Dee said, sniffing.

Sophie could spy the imminent collapse of whatever reserve of strength her friend still had left. "Let's get out of here. Some fresh air and privacy. Just for a few moments." She took her hand. "Come on. We'll figure this out."

Delia sniffled behind her as Sophie looked for the most direct but private exit. She sent a steady stream of silent apolo-gies to Simon, wherever he was, for once again screwing up her assignment. Clearly she was not cut out for the job, but that didn't keep her from feeling horrible about it. "Here," she said, spying an exit door in the rear of the room. Praying it didn't set off alarms, she pushed through it, and a few seconds later, spied another door leading to a side exit from the building. This one was guarded, but the uniformed gentleman took one look at the obvious distress on Delia's face and opened the door for them. "Ladies," he said, nodding. "You'll have to re-enter at the front."

"That's fine. No problem," Sophie said, tugging Dee out behind her. "Thank you."

She saw him radio something, and assumed it was just to alert security that he'd let two guests out the side door, but Dee had given up completely and started crying in earnest, so she couldn't follow more of what the guard was saying as the door closed behind them.

"Over here," she said, spying a metal bench seat. "Come on, sit down. Tell me what's going on."

In between sniffles and choking back tears, Delia said, "I—I overheard them. Talking. About me."

"Who? His sisters? His mother? You know they haven't come around yet, but they will when you show them what you're made of. It will take time, but you'll win in the end, I know you."

Delia lifted her tear-and-mascara streaked face to look directly at Sophie. "Not them. I know they hate me. Adam. I heard him. With my own ears."

"Who was he talking to? His friends? His mother?"

"I don't think he ever loved me, Soph," she said, her voice wobbling and a fresh wave of tears brimming over to trickle down her cheeks. "Adam—he was talking to his best friend, Trevor, his best man. He got into town last night with his wife, and I didn't know he'd stopped by. I inadvertently walked in on their conversation, but they were out on the balcony, they didn't know I was there. I—I heard him." She buried her face in her hands.

"What was he saying? Because men get cold feet. You had cold feet, remember?" Sophie couldn't believe she was supporting Adam, of all people, but she was trying to keep up with what Delia wanted and needed, and, right now, it seemed like she needed to believe this wedding was a good idea. Lord knew Sophie had wasted enough breath trying to convince her it wasn't. Now wasn't the time for I-told-you-so's.

"Oh, he wants to marry me."

"Okay," Sophie said brightly, trying to grasp for any scrap of good news. "That's a positive. What else did he say?"

"Trevor said he was surprised that Adam chose me given my lack of pedigree. That he couldn't believe Arlene was letting him get away with it. And—and then, Adam said…" She sniffled again, then took a deep breath and blurted, "Adam laughed—laughed!—and said he's doing it, marrying me, as a way to get even with his mother. Th-that he's only marrying me to drive a wedge between them so he can get some breath-breathing room." Delia looked up again, anguish clear on her face. "He's using me, Soph. I'm just a tool he's using to get out from under Mommy-dearest's rule. He plans on shoving me at his mother to keep her occupied and off his back. He—he even said he'd knock me up—his words—if that's what it took to get some space."

Sophie didn't know what to say. That was the hard part. Because nothing her friend was saying surprised her in the least. "At least you found out now, Dee. Before you said I do." Sophie held her and rubbed her back, and let her get it out.

"He—he even told Trevor that he had no plans to remain faith-faithful to me!" she squeaked. "For all I know, he's already cheating on me. And Trevor, he just laughed, and said, 'Join the club, buddy. Join the club.'" Delia sat up. "Who *are* these people, Sophie? And where in the hell do they get off toying with others like this? I know you told me, but he was so sincere, and so handsome, and so willing, I was just swept away. But he—he…he never…" She broke down again.

"I think he did care for you, Delia. I don't know when his plan kicked in about his mother, but I don't think he chose you in some cold, calculating way." Actually, Sophie wouldn't be surprised if he'd done exactly that. "But now that you know where he stands, what are you going to do?"

"That's just it!" she exclaimed on a sob. "What *can* I do?"

"Um…call the wedding off? I mean, Dee, you can't marry the guy now. You know that."

"I don't know anything. What I know is that they've spent millions on this wedding. *Millions,* Soph. I know it's hard to comprehend, but seriously, the money alone… And then there's Arlene and her standing and how it would look. Oh, can you imagine, the 'cocktail waitress' ditching her son? Can you imagine?"

Sophie's lips twitched, and then she smiled, and then she laughed. "I'm sorry, really, I am, but, oh my God, Delia, can you imagine it? Because I can. In fact, I can't think of a better way for this to end. With you in the driver's seat, calling all the shots. If I thought you could pull it off, I'd have you ditch him at the altar. He deserves the public humiliation for all he's put you through, and I don't just mean his little speech to Trevor. Hell, you could call Trevor out, too. And Arlene. Right there at the pulpit, with camera recorders blazing."

She immediately started to apologize, but then she saw Delia's lips twitch, and then she was spluttering, and laughing, and then they were both laughing until anyone passing by would think perhaps they needed an intervention of some sort.

But it was cathartic, and healing, and it just felt really damn good.

"I'm so sorry I didn't listen to you," Delia said, when they finally stopped long enough to draw in a breath. "It's like I've been inhabited by another person all this time. Like I've been above myself, watching this happen, and being alternately amazed that I was getting to be Cinderella at the ball, but wondering who in the hell this person was I was becoming." She stared at Sophie, heedless now of the black streaks on her face, and the red, splotchy cheeks. "I can't marry him, Sophie. I can't believe I ever wanted to marry him."

"I know, Dee. I know." She took her friend in her arms and hugged her tight. "I'll do whatever I can to help. I'll be there with you when you tell him, whatever you think you need. We're all behind you, you know."

"Oh God, you must all think I'm a total fool."

"No, we think you wanted the fairy tale as much as we wanted it for you. We just didn't want to see you hurt, that's all. It's a lot easier to see the big picture when you're not the focus of all of it. We were just worried about you. We love you. You know that."

She nodded and snuffled again. "What am I going to do, Soph? How am I going to tell him? I wish I could do the altar thing, he deserves it, but I don't think I have it in me."

"I know. I think you're just going to have to sit down with him, and tell him you can't go through with it." Sophie thought about how controlling Adam was, how mad he was likely to be that his big plan was being thwarted, not to mention how he was going to look in all of it. "On the other hand, maybe you shouldn't be completely alone when you tell him. Maybe you should tell the whole family."

The horror that immediately leaped into her friend's eyes had her quickly backpedaling. "Okay, okay, maybe not a good idea."

"They'd railroad me, Sophie. I don't think I could stand up to all of them. They don't like me, and they don't want me in the family, but they're committed to this now and there is no backing out. I don't know if I could take them on collectively." She sighed. "Maybe it's easier to just go through with it, then live with it until I can't take it anymore, and file for divorce. I mean, at least I know what I'm getting into now."

"You can't be serious."

"I don't know what I am. Except exhausted. I've been running on fumes for what feels like an eternity."

"What you need is a good night's sleep. Away from the Wingate influence." Sophie pulled her tiny clutch purse onto her lap. "Why don't you stay at my place tonight." She handed Delia her apartment key.

"Why are you giving me the key? Won't you be there?"

She thought of Simon, and the very strong possibility that by choosing to help her friend rather than help steal a priceless emerald, she might have very well screwed up her chance at the future she'd been allowing herself to envision for the past few days. "I—I'm not sure."

Delia narrowed her puffy eyes. "What aren't you telling me?"

"Trust me, you have enough on your plate without me cluttering it up more."

"Sophie," she said warningly. And she sounded so much like the best friend Sophie had thought she'd lost forever, she wanted to hug her and hold on tight.

"Later. I'll tell you everything, I promise. But…just let me say that I'm far more sensitive to what it's like to be making decisions while inside the whirlwind and it's not easy. Nothing is simple."

"No. It's definitely not."

She pressed the key into her friend's hand. "Do you want me to come stay with you?" She smiled. "Keep you from jumping? Buy some almond rocca? I have ice cream in the freezer."

Delia smiled through a fresh sheen of tears. "No. I think I need to be completely by myself for once. And do a lot of thinking. I know I need to end this. I can't marry him. I just have to decide how I'm going to do it."

"If you change your mind, if you need backup, or just some bolstering, or someone to bounce ideas and thoughts off of…"

She grinned. "Or just someone to have a plain old bitchfest with, call my cell and I'll be right there."

"Maybe after I tell him," Delia said, a smile wavering through the tears. "I will definitely need some artificial sweetening by then, for sure."

"Sugar high, here we come."

Sophie stood and pulled her friend up by the hands. "Come on. I'll sneak around front and direct a cab here to the side of the building for you."

"What about Adam?"

Sophie wanted to tell her he'd probably hardly miss her, as taken as he was with Marcelina, but what she said was, "I'll tell him you didn't feel well, your stomach or something."

"He'll demand to know where I went."

"Yes, well, maybe it's time he stopped having the right to know your whereabouts every single second."

"He'll go crazy trying to find me."

Sophie smiled. "Yes, he will."

Delia smiled then, too. "Right. You can just tell him you have no idea where I went." Her shoulders straightened and her chin notched up a bit higher. "I hope he has a very, very long night ahead of him."

And Sophie knew right then her friend was going to be just fine.

16

SIMON WATCHED AS ADAM and Marcelina started their slow trek toward what he assumed was the bar for a drink. Glancing back, he also noted that Delia and Sophie had vanished from Tolliver's immediate circle and had disappeared somewhere. He started making a circuitous route toward the bar himself, hoping that Sophie spied him and steered clear. For safety's sake—hers more than his—he didn't need anyone at the event to put the two of them together. As much as he wanted to meet Sophie's friend, this was not the time or place for introductions.

He was still impressed with how well and quickly Sophie had managed to get her job done. She'd gotten into Tolliver's circle quite easily. He'd been a little worried that she might be out of her league and not fully realize who she was dealing with, but she seemed to have held her own. He'd recognized her friend Delia and Adam Wingate immediately—hard not to when the two lovebirds were being splashed across every local paper and magazine—and had worried that their sudden appearance might cause problems. But moments later, Marcelina had been successfully cut from the pack, allowing him the kind of unmonitored access he could have only dreamed of.

As he moved closer, he scanned the crowd around the

groom-to-be and the supermodel, but didn't see any obvious hired muscle. Which was just as well. The level of security covering the gala was already at an all-time high for what would be typical of events of this caliber. He didn't know if that was Tolliver's doing, so he didn't have to have hulks shadowing his and Marcelina's every move during the gala itself, but he would certainly bet on it.

He worked his way closer, keeping an eye behind him as well, but Tolliver was still ensconced in his throng of admirers and hadn't so much as looked Marcelina's way, as far as he could tell. He was a paranoid man where it came to security, but Simon also knew he was rather smug about his power and control. Once safely inside the confines of the Institute, surrounded by security, and relishing his place as the star of the gala, he was certain Tolliver was quite happy reveling in the attention he—and his collection—were receiving. The more coverage he could gain out of it, the better. And having Marcelina and the emerald being escorted around the room on the arm of the other feted star of the night—Adam Wingate—was like double-teaming the event.

"Well," Simon muttered, "we'll see what we can do to ruin that for you." He thought of Guinn, reading all the press coverage and knowing that not only had Tolliver found a way to snatch his heritage from him, but now his pride and dignity as well, by wrongfully claiming Guinn's birthright as his own for all the world to see. He might not be able to do anything about what was in the cases, but it was the Shay that Guinn wanted more than anything else, and what Simon had personally kept him from having. One way or the other, it was going back to London, back to Guinn.

He gave a quick scan of the room, but still no sight of Sophie or Delia. He prayed she wouldn't suddenly turn up, and was trusting that he had it under control, but wished there had been some way to keep in contact during the event. Phones, cameras and all other recording devices had been banned from the gala floor and were being held in the security office for those who couldn't leave them at home.

Adam had just handed Marcelina a drink as Simon started to close in. She wouldn't recognize him, and he hoped he might be able to distract the model long enough to entice her to a more private place before she headed back to Tolliver's side. As for the higher profile Adam, he figured he could find a way to shame the man into going back to his bride-to-be, leaving Marcelina in his care. At least, that was the plan.

But it was immediately thwarted when Adam didn't lead Marcelina back into the throng, but took the opportunity himself for a more private conversation. Simon wanted to clap Adam on the back for inadvertently doing the hard work for him, but wasn't as certain of his plan to dismiss the blond Adonis if there were no crowds around to help ensure the guy's good behavior.

He saw them duck into a display and had to do some nimble dodging to wind his way into the same area while not losing sight of them. Most of the guests were in the larger, more open rooms, but there were a number of couples wandering the outer exhibits as well. Many looked more interested in each other than the artwork on display, but that could work to Simon's advantage. Later, when the emerald went missing, if people were questioned, hopefully no one would remember him.

He finally turned the last corner…only to discover no one there. There was no way out of this particular area without backtracking, so he wasn't sure where they could have gone. Then he heard the giggling. And it sounded remarkably like what Sophie had described after bearing witness to the shower scene in Tolliver's suite.

He casually used his body to block the entrance to the small display area, keeping other wandering couples from entering…and giving the wandering hands of the couple he had now targeted as being behind one of the display panels a chance to get further involved with one another.

The giggles diminished, replaced by a short groan or two.... Simon waited a bit longer, until he heard a bit of a scuffle, saw the panel vibrate, and one of the movable walls wobble a bit as body parts bumped, and more giggles were finally stifled by a series of soft moans.

Checking to make sure no one was in the general vicinity of the area, Simon moved closer to the shaky panel, until he could hear the unmistakable sounds of two people climbing quite rapidly toward...completion.

Perfect time then, to poke his head around the corner. "Hullo, there. I wasn't aware this was an interactive exhibit. Well done." He stepped around the partition and clapped his hands slowly.

There was a short, stifled scream as Marcelina clung to Adam, who had his tux pants around his ankles and Marcelina's legs wrapped around his hips. "Get the hell out of here," Adam barked.

Not, Simon noted, doing the least bit to help preserve the modesty, much less the reputation, of his famous partner-in-amore. "Why, I'd be more than happy to. Just as soon as I relieve your partner there of another piece of attire."

Marcelina swiveled as best she could to get away from Simon's reaching hands, but as her back was closest to him, there was little either of them could do without risking getting tangled up in the pool of Adam's trousers, falling over and knocking the partition over in a sprawling display, revealing their furtive activities.

Thankful for her upswept hairstyle, Simon unclipped the emeralds and slid them from Marcelina's neck before she could do anything to stop him.

"Wait," she screeched. "Thief! You can't just take them! Tolly will kill me! "

"Oh, but I can. And they aren't Tolliver's to begin with. Ask him about it. Tell him Guinn sends his regards. And I don't think you'll want to shout for the guards. At least not until you've gotten your pants up there, mate," he added, nodding to Adam.

"You'll pay for this! I'll have half of Chicago after you," Adam threatened, trying to disentangle himself from Marcelina, whose bunched-up gown was caught on his tux jacket.

"And here it will take only two people to bring you down," Simon said as he slipped the emeralds into a specially prepared pocket inside his tuxedo. "I imagine your fiancée won't take the news kindly. Or worse—" he smiled "—your mother."

Adam blanched, but quickly regrouped. "Tell a single soul and I'll have you hunted down," he called out as Simon waited for a gap in guests and quickly slipped out of the display area.

"You do that," he murmured. "And we'll just see who pays the bigger price."

He felt the weight of the emeralds thumping against his chest, keeping time with the pounding of his heart as he made his way through the exhibit, plotting just how he was going to make his escape. With the heightened security, it was going to be quite the challenge, but given he was carrying the only piece on display tonight not wired to an alarm system, other than the mouth of the woman who'd been wearing them, he had about a sixty-second window to find an exit and get himself on the other side of it, before all hell broke loose.

Quite likely, as soon as Marcelina told someone the emeralds were missing, the building would be put on lockdown, and each of the guests, as well as the premises, would be thoroughly searched. He couldn't let that happen while he was still in it. Not only would it forever keep the Shay from Guinn's hands, but it would put his freedom in jeopardy, and, most importantly, Sophie's, as her connection to him would surely come out. Probably by her own volition.

She was determined and strong, but too softhearted for this kind of thing. He should have known better, should have known— "Ooph."

He'd rounded a corner...and run directly into Sophie's arms. "No," he said, sounding as frantic as he felt. "No, no, no. You can't be here. Not now."

"Simon," she said, trying to regroup from their collision. "What—where did Adam and—"

"Behind me."

She glanced down at where his hand was over his heart, holding his jacket tight to his body. "You did it!"

"I have to get out of here."

"Oh, right! Okay! What can I do?"

"Not be seen with me. By anyone. Sophie, I should have never—"

"Shh," she said. "I love you, Simon. What can I do to buy you more time?"

He lifted his head. "What did you just say?"

"Go!" she said, shoving at him. "I'll buy you more time."

"Sophie, no—don't go back—"

But she'd already headed back into the exhibits, and it was too late to go after her. All he could do was exactly what she'd told him to do.

Run.

And pray like hell she knew what she was doing.

"I love you, too, Sophie Maplethorpe," he said under his breath as he made his way closer to the crowds, trying like hell to calm himself down and look like he hadn't just stolen a priceless gemstone. "And, as God is my witness, if we get through this without doing hard labor for twenty-to-life, I'm going to marry you and never let either one of us break the law, ever again."

He took a deep breath as he entered the main area, forced himself to slow down, then lifted a glass of champagne from a passing tray, downing the entire contents in one gulp. He put the glass down on another passing tray, then straightened his shoulders and did his best impression of a man casually enjoying the evening's festivities, smiling and nodding as he passed this group or that, but winding his way toward the exit with purpose. He could feel the clock ticking down like a giant bomb about to go off.

He had the exit door in sight when he heard a woman's voice raise quite distinctly above the murmur of conversation and shout, "Adam! How could you! And with Marcelina?"

He smiled and ducked his head as conversations fell silent and folks started to shift toward the back of the exhibit hall, where it appeared some kind of drama was unfolding. All he heard as he moved quickly in the other direction was people murmuring things like, "Do you think it's Adam Wingate?" and, "I saw him with Marcelina earlier." "Men, all of them, cheating bastards," muttered another aging socialite. "Don't I know it," said another. "And his fiancée, she seemed so sweet. Beautiful girl."

Simon had no idea how long he had before the part about the emeralds going missing was added to the evening's entertainment, but he planned to be long gone by then. As he came close to the entrance, and the guard planted there, the mayhem behind him was rolling into a full-scale "incident." The guard was on his radio, trying to get a report.

Simon caught his eye and, despite feeling like he was going to have a heart attack, he grinned. "Can you believe it? Bloke is rich as Croesus and engaged to the most gorgeous blonde you've ever seen. Caught with his pants down behind some display in the back. I hear it was with one of your supermodels. Some guys get all the luck, ay, mate?"

The guard smiled and chuckled. "Hey, you take what you can get, when you can get it, you know?"

"Yes," Simon said, nodding as the guard held the door open for him, his attention once more diverted as someone squawked to him on his radio. "I do, indeed."

"I told you," she said, openly smug. "Now, help me get

17

"WHAT DO YOU MEAN, YOU QUIT?"

"Well, it was really a preemptive move, since I'm pretty sure when it gets out that I've spoken up on Delia's behalf to any press who will listen to me, I was going to be canned anyway."

"Sophie—"

"Simon. Where are you? Should we be talking? Is it safe? I've been worried sick, waiting to hear from you."

There was silence, during which Sophie grew more nervous. "Wait, this isn't your 'one phone call' is it? Where are you, how much is bail? Oh God, is there bail?"

"I'm a free man, no worries."

She collapsed back on her bed, where she'd been holed up pretty much exclusively for the past forty-eight hours. "Thank God. Was Guinn shocked? Did—"

"Sophie, we can talk about all that later. Where are you?"

"In my apartment, why?"

"Then why haven't you opened your door?"

"What?" She shot up on the bed. "I've been hounded by the press and every tabloid on the planet, maybe some from off planet, given the types of scum that have been trolling

my apartment door. Why?" She was already scrambling off
the bed and racing to her front door, heedless of the fact that
she looked like hell and her apartment looked even worse.
She and Delia had spent twenty-four of those last forty-eight
hours hiding from the world and re-cementing the bonds of
their sisterhood. It had entailed a great deal of sugar and not
a small amount of alcohol.

There was a small tap on the door just as she skidded to a
halt in front of it. "Who's there?" she asked, her heart in her
throat.

"Housekeeping."

"Don't tease me, you haven't seen this place."

"I'm pretty handy with a mop. I don't cook half badly
either."

"You're hired." She hurried through five different locks,
then flung the door open and flung herself into Simon's waiting arms.

He spun her through the door and kicked it shut, his mouth
already on hers. "Bed?" he murmured against her lips.

"That way," she managed, flinging one arm in the general
direction. "Careful, it's a bit messy."

"All I see is you."

He tripped, stumbled and banged them both into the
doorframe before managing to get them to her bed. "My God,
was there a raid on your place?"

"I thought all you saw was me," she teased, thinking she'd
never seen anything better in her whole life.

"I am looking at you."

She swatted him. "Very funny. Thank God you know I
clean up well, right?"

"True."

She pulled him down and held on for dear life. "I was so
afraid," she said, her voice shaking now, which made no sense
since he was finally here, safe in her arms.

"Of?"

"That I'd never see you again. I've been holed up here with Delia, dealing with the press, the Wingates, everything, and there hasn't been even a whisper about the emerald going missing, and it's— I wasn't sure if maybe I just hallucinated you."

He lifted his head. "Did you tell Delia? About us?"

She nodded. "I had to, Simon. I was going crazy."

"What did she say?"

Sophie smiled. "That I'm crazy. She's one to talk, right? But it helped. It helped us both get through."

"Crazy in love?" he asked, and surprised her with the vulnerability she spied in his eyes.

"That crazy," she said, so happy she could finally say it again, tell him, show him. Her heart felt like it was going to burst now that he was here. Then it was her turn to be a bit shy. "You?"

"Completely. Head over heels. Gone. Besotted. Out of my head. Yours."

Her smile spread. "Keep going. I'm liking this."

He framed her face, and his expression grew more serious. "I'm sorry," he said. "About…everything. I've been worried sick about you, too, but I had to make sure, for both of us, that things were taken care of before I contacted you."

She nodded, but her eyes were glassy now. "I know. I mean, I was hoping, anyway. I— It's all been so insane, Simon. I missed you."

"I missed you, too. I wanted you with me. Crazy indeed, for a bloke who has been on his own as long as I have, but it didn't seem right, you not being there. But I've been following everything. You didn't have to quit, you know. They had no grounds."

"I couldn't work for them anymore, anyway. I loved the hotel itself, and the staff, but Delia was right. If I couldn't back the family themselves, then how could I justify working for them? And working in such a big operation really isn't what

I want to do. It was just the only way I could see to make the money I needed, as quickly as possible."

"Then I think you did the right thing. Leaving, I mean."

She smiled, even as she sniffed and he wiped the corners of her eyes with his thumbs. "So, the good news is, I don't have to stay in Chicago. In fact, Delia and I were discussing relocating. As far away from here as possible."

"Have you now?" he asked, a spark of consideration dawning in his eyes.

"When the news hit and the wedding was called off, even though Delia came through it all as the wronged heroine of the tale, it's still been incredibly hard on her."

"I can only imagine."

"She's been holed up in her place when she hasn't been holed up here with me. We're both not sure what to do next, but we really don't want to do it here. And I know you said you'd be willing to move here, and it's central and all, but I really think we want something smaller, more rural, I think."

"I've an idea about that," Simon said.

"Do you?" She sighed in relief. "I thought you'd be upset."

"Why in the world would I be upset? I don't want you to be anywhere you don't want to be. And that includes being with me."

She held him tightly. "This is the one place I know I want to be. I know it sounds crazy to say this, given all that has happened since I met you, but you're the one thing that's keeping me grounded and sane through all this. Knowing you're there for me. That you believe in me. How nuts is that?"

"As nutty as I am, apparently," he said, and kissed her. The kiss didn't stop this time, and grew until he rolled her over to her back and covered her body with his. "I miss you, Sophie."

"What happened?" she asked him. "There was never a single word in the news about it being taken. I couldn't believe it. Not a single word from Tolliver, either, other than the announcement that by mutual consent, his donated collection would be removed from the Institute. Everyone assumed it had to do with his distaste and perhaps embarrassment over what happened during the gala. I didn't know what to think."

"Tolliver is a very private man, who only likes to make grand, public gestures when it suits him best. When Marcelina mentioned that it was someone named Guinn who took the emerald—I just told her that Guinn sent his regards and she misunderstood, but it served the purpose—Tolliver was on the next flight back to London."

"But—where were you?"

"I've never left Chicago."

"What?" She pushed him off her and sat up. "And you didn't tell me? Where is the emerald? Oh my God, don't tell me you didn't—"

"Wait, wait just a minute before you go running off. Though, might I say, you're quite adorable when you do."

She smacked away his hand, but was already smiling and chuckling when he pulled her back beneath him and trapped her there with the weight of his leg over hers as he shifted to his side. "Tell me everything. Don't leave anything out."

"Without knowing exactly what was happening at the gala, I couldn't risk trying to get it out of the country. I thought about Canada, but instead I simply contacted Guinn and told him I had it."

"He's elderly, you said. And infirm, right? So, how—"

"He sent someone to retrieve it for him. And he was very, very grateful."

"So…he has it. It's safe."

Simon nodded.

"And you made peace. With him. And yourself."

He nodded again, and smiled.

"And Tolliver?"

"Will have to duke it out with Guinn if he wants to continue the battle for ownership. He didn't come forward in the press with any of it, which only confirms my suspicions that his so-called proof would prove to be false if more closely and expertly examined. Fortunately, if you could call it that, Marcelina's indiscretion gave him the cover he needed to withdraw quietly from the scene and from the public. And being a continent away certainly isn't hurting, either, as the press will die down without him around to fuel it."

"So...it's over?"

"For now. But if and when Tolliver decides to go after Guinn or the necklace again—and I believe he will at some point, he doesn't give up so easily—I won't be involved. The Shay is with the man who should have it, and that's where it ends with me."

"So, that's it, then. You're truly out of it?"

"Job done. And done well, I might add. Brilliant diversion, by the way."

She smiled. "Thank you. Just please tell me that your job doesn't usually include this sort of retrieving. Because you know how I am, I'm going to want to help, but I really don't think there is a great advantage in having me be involved in any way on cases like this in the future."

"Agreed."

She sighed in relief. "Good."

"On all of it. I find myself curiously disinclined to take on another case at the moment, either."

"Why? Because you'd have to go back to London? Because that was part of what I was thinking about—"

"No, because it would take me away from you."

"I could go with you," she said hopefully. "Do you need an assistant? Not on the cases, exactly, but helping you research them, maybe?"

"You don't want to be doing that. It's not your passion."

She stroked his cheek. "But it is yours, Simon."

"Which is why I've been thinking."

"Have you now?" She smiled and her heart started to pick up pace again. "About?"

"It's been a while since I've been home. And while you are right, I do have a passion for helping folks, for unearthing things, I've been thinking maybe it's time to scale back a little, be a bit more local in my focus."

"Local to…?"

"Do you have a passport?"

She nodded.

"Would you like to come home with me, Sophie? See my father's place, see Hawke's Bay? I've been thinking, maybe it wouldn't be such a bad place for a small inn. And I could open up an office, perhaps oversee a bit more closely the workings of the vineyard."

"But you don't want—"

"No, I don't want to run the winery. But it's not a bad way to make contacts for the job I do love. I could also look into helping at the university. Maybe get back to my real love."

"Wouldn't that mean traveling again?"

"I was thinking as a teacher this time."

She smiled, trembling now, unable to believe what she was hearing. "Could it be so simple as all that?"

He laughed. "I don't think there is a single thing simple about any part of our relationship so far. Except falling in love with you. That was remarkably easy." He rolled on top of her, framed her face with his hands and looked deeply into her eyes. "I do love you, Sophie Maplethorpe. Will you come home with me? And, if you want, after seeing it, make a home with me there? If it's not to your liking, we can hunt the world over until we find the right place. I'm good at finding things, you know."

"And thank God for it. Because you found me." She kissed him. "Take me home, Simon. It's been a grand adventure since I met you. And I can't wait to find out what happens next."

Epilogue

Two years later

"WE'VE BOOKED THE TWO SUITES and the small loft space through the summer. But there is a small problem."

Sophie looked up from the books she'd been poring over, trying to decide if it was too soon to think about the upgrades she wanted to make to the front parlor and library. The Lassiter Inn had only just celebrated its second anniversary, but business had never been better.

"Well, that's why I hired you. To solve problems." She smiled at Mick. "What is it this time? Sheep got loose again and into the orchard? Guests are asking again about stomping their own wine? Because this is New Zealand, not Italy, and our grapes—"

"No, that's not it. It's just, I have this gentleman at the front desk and he's demanding to see the proprietress of the inn. I believe those were his exact words. He's not settling for me, and Dee has her hands full in the kitchen, getting dinner ready for our guests. Roast duck tonight." He sighed in deep appreciation. Not unusual for any of Delia's fare.

Sophie closed the book on the pile of receipts she'd been tallying. "Whatever could this man want that you can't provide him help with?"

Mick disappeared from view and Simon's head full of tousled dark hair filled her view instead. "He's an amazing majordomo and Brian would hire him away to run the winery single-handedly if he weren't afraid of you, so far be it from me to diminish Mick's skills in any way."

"However, here you are, going over his head to the boss and interrupting her very busy day."

He stepped into the room, and she spied the picnic basket in his hands. "I was thinking perhaps I could interrupt it on a somewhat more involved scale?"

"Were you?" She was already pushing her chair back.

"And though Mick is going to be involved in the discussion, as you have the final say, I thought it best to bribe—er, that is, deal with you directly."

She had rounded her desk, but paused and leaned back on it. "Okay. So, what is it I need to give my final say on?"

He slipped his hand inside the basket lid and drew out two plane tickets. "Seeing as Mick could also probably run this inn single-handedly, at least for a short while, and Dee chases anyone who even thinks of commandeering her kitchen out with a spoon, I was hoping perhaps the boss lady could accompany me on a university speaking engagement."

"To?"

"London."

Her eyes lit up and her heart skipped a beat. "We haven't been to the flat there in a long time."

"Not since the honeymoon."

"Nope. Not since."

He fanned the tickets out further. "There might be another leg to the trip."

"To?"

"Philadelphia. It's been a while since you've seen your family, and I was thinking—"

She flew across the office into his arms. "You were thinking you missed out on my cousin's Philly cheesesteak and were hoping to sneak the recipe back for Dee."

"Well, that, too."

"When do we leave?"

"Can we at least pretend to have a picnic before you decide?" He hitched her up against him with one arm and wiggled his eyebrows. "I packed a blanket."

"Did you."

"I did."

"And might there be some wine in that basket."

"There might be."

"Then what are you waiting for, Mr. Lassiter?"

"You, Mrs. Lassiter. In fact, I've been waiting for you my whole life."

He dropped the basket on the chair, and kicked the door shut.

It was a while before they got to the wine.

* * * * *

COMING NEXT MONTH

Available July 27, 2010

#555 TWICE THE TEMPTATION
Cara Summers
Forbidden Fantasies/Encounters

#556 CLAIMED!
Vicki Lewis Thompson
Sons of Chance

#557 THE RENEGADE
Rhonda Nelson
Men Out of Uniform

#558 THE HEAT IS ON
Jill Shalvis
American Heroes

#559 CATCHING HEAT
Lisa Renee Jones

#560 DOUBLE PLAY
Joanne Rock
The Wrong Bed

REQUEST YOUR FREE BOOKS!

2 FREE NOVELS
PLUS 2
FREE GIFTS!

HARLEQUIN®

Blaze™

Red-hot reads!

HB10R

HARLEQUIN®

A Romance

FOR EVERY MOOD™

Spotlight on

Heart & Home

Heartwarming romances
where love can happen
right when you least expect it.

See the next page to enjoy a sneak peek
from Harlequin® American Romance®,
a Heart and Home series.

Five hunky Texas single fathers—five stories from Cathy Gillen Thacker's LONE STAR DADS *miniseries. Here's an excerpt from the latest,* THE MOMMY PROPOSAL *from Harlequin American Romance.*

"I hear you work miracles," Nate Hutchinson drawled. Brooke Mitchell had just stepped into his lavishly appointed office in downtown Fort Worth, Texas.

"Sometimes, I do." Brooke smiled and took the sexy financier's hand in hers, shook it briefly.

"Good." Nate looked her straight in the eye. "Because I'm in need of a home makeover—fast. The son of an old friend is coming to live with me."

She was still tingling from the feel of his warm palm. "Temporarily or permanently?"

"If all goes according to plan, I'll adopt Landry by summer's end."

Brooke had heard the founder of Nate Hutchinson Financial Services was eligible, wealthy and generous to a fault. She hadn't known he was in the market for a family, but she supposed she shouldn't be surprised. But Brooke had figured a man as successful and handsome as Nate would want one the old-fashioned way. *Not that this was any of her business...*

"So what's the child like?" she asked crisply, trying not to think how the marine-blue of Nate's dress shirt deepened the hue of his eyes.

"I don't know." Nate took a seat behind his massive antique mahogany desk. He relaxed against the smooth leather of the chair. "I've never met him."

"Yet you've invited this kid to live with you permanently?"

"It's complicated. But I'm sure it's going to be fine."

Obviously Nate Hutchinson knew as little about teenage

boys as he did about decorating. But that wasn't her problem. Finding a way to do the assignment without getting the least bit emotionally involved was.

Find out how a young boy brings Nate and Brooke together in THE MOMMY PROPOSAL, coming August 2010 from Harlequin American Romance.

HARLEQUIN® *Blaze*™

THE HEAT IS ON
by
Jill Shalvis

The attraction between Bella and
Detective Madden is undeniable.
But can a few wild encounters
turn into love?

Don't miss this hot read.

*Available in August
where books are sold.*
